He left his suite and looked up and down the corridor. No one was in sight. He walked quickly to the suite next to his and went in. The door was unlocked.

She was sitting on the couch. Her face was intent, her very blue eyes staring wildly. For a moment, Rocky's warning about some of the people who came to Satellite City flashed through his mind.

"I didn't expect it to be you," she said. "I paid fifty thousand pseudo-dollars for this—and I'm glad it's going to be a pig like you!"

Her hand darted into her bag, then came out with a laser pistol. She held it in both hands, aimed for his chest, and pulled the trigger.

A tiny beam of deadly light lanced out.

World traveler, expert observer of the human condition, Mack Reynolds has been a world famous Science Fiction writer for more than two decades. In fact, of all the writers published in the leading SF magazines, *Galaxy* and *If,* a poll conducted among the readers put the stories of Mack Reynolds consistently higher than any other. Perhaps it is because his stories have an uncanny way of discussing *now* the questions that will concern everyone ten or twenty years later.

SATELLITE CITY

by

MACK REYNOLDS

WILDSIDE PRESS

SATELLITE CITY

Copyright © 1975 by Mack Reynolds

PART ONE

I

He stood in the Place de France and looked about. It was the first time he had ever been in this town but he had read about it, as everyone has read about it. In this case, since he had been old enough to care about the romanticism of far and exotic lands. To his right was Pasteur Boulevard, once the underground banking center of the world. Directly ahead of him was the Rue de la Liberte, leading down to the Grand Socco and to the Medina and Kasbah, the old Moroccan part of town. And from where he stood he could look out over the Straits of Hercules, with Spain beyond, and a misty view of Gibralter, undoubtedly the most picturesque landfall in the world.

Tangier had changed little in the last fifty years, he assumed. In fact, he suspected that, compared to the rest of the world, it had changed little in the past century or two, and in many respects, in the last millennium. Surely, the Riff in their vivid costumes of hand woven, embroideried red and white stripes, must have looked much the same as when Tarik first stormed across the straits with his Moslem armies.

So much for nostalgic reflections on yesteryear and the slowness of change in the world of Islam. He could plan to go down into the Medina and then up to the Kasbah later and do a little sampling of the nightlife—dine on cous cous, watch the emasculated dancing boys, smoke kif, and wince at the blare of Moroccan musical instruments. It was all in character. But for now he had business.

He strolled on down Boulevard Pasteur into the European, or rather Western, part of town, finding it difficult to realize that he wasn't in Nice or some other ultramodern city of Common Europe. ·The electro-steamers were probably privately owned, he realized, rather than being auto-taxis. In fact, he understood that automated roads, not to speak of streets in town, had not as yet come to Morocco. But then, the number of vehicles wasn't such that automated traffic was the necessity it was in either the United States of the Americas or even the Soviet Complex. Most of the women in this Europeanized section were in the latest of fashion from Paris, Budapest or Tokyo. The men were prosperous and conservative in their styles from Greater London, or Hong Kong. Even the poodles, clipped to within an inch of their lives, radiated prosperity and arrogance.

The Satellite City Authority offices occupied a whole building, towering a full twenty stories. Unconsciously, he let his glance go up into the heavens and could make out Satellite City itself, twenty-two thousand miles high, so he understood, but larger than Venus to the naked eye.

The lobby was swank and ostentatious to the point of having a bank of three live receptionists, rather than computerized screens.

He came up to the first of them and she rewarded him with a smile so flashing that one could have thought he was about to date her.

She said, "Oui, Monsieur?"

He said, "My French is atrocious. Do you speak English?"

"But, of course, sir." She had the slight British plus New England American accent that seems to result from learning the language through Berlitz rather than in the home, or in either British or American schools.

He hesitated before saying, "I have a . . . project in mind that involves my going to Satellite City."

"Of course, sir." She checked a screen before her. "Fräulein Muller is free. That would be Office Fourteen, on the 3rd Floor. Your name, please?"

"Brown."

The receptionist said things into the screen, and then gave him the benefit of the dazzling smile again. "If you'll just take elevator D."

He took elevator D to the 3rd Floor and had no trouble finding Office Fourteen. He stood before the door's identity screen and said, "Mr. Brown to see Fräulein Muller."

The door opened and he entered. Fräulein Muller was there behind a desk and managed to look both efficient and feminine. The femininity was out of place. The fräulein was getting along in years and should have been a frau by this time, assuming anyone would have wished to wed such efficiency. She was at least in her mid-forties and looked as though she had kept at a high pitch of executive activity for at least a quarter of a century of that. Her face was innocent of make-up which was an indication of good sense on her part. Cosmetics would have availed her naught.

She motioned to a chair, briskly, and said, "Yes, Mr. Brown?" She was not the linguist the receptionist had proved. Her accent had a heavy Teutonic quality.

Mr. Brown said, "I have a rather unique reason for wishing to visit Satellite City. A very confidential reason.

7

I would want as few persons as possible to know about it."

She looked at him carefully, took in his expensive garb, including the very earnest shoes which had cost him a hundred pseudo-dollars in London.

She said, "One moment, please," and consulted one of her several desk screens.

"That would be our Senor Byass," she said, after pursing her lips.

She flicked on another screen and spoke into it briefly, then turned back to him with what was probably meant to be a smile, and wasn't; not in his book.

"Senor Byass will be able to see you immediately. He is in Suite Three on the 20th Floor. Please take elevator A, it is the sole one that goes to the ultimate reaches of the Satellite City Authority Building."

Elevator A was the only one in the bank of elevators that had an identity screen on it. The man who called himself Brown stood before it.

The screen said, the robot voice unctuous, as computer voices went, "Your name, please?"

Brown gave it and the screen said, "You are expected, Mr. Brown," and the door opened.

The Satellite City Authority Building was modern and very well conceived but the Floor 20 outdid itself. Off hand, Brown couldn't remember ever seeing anything quite so palatial, even in Greater Washington.

If there was an identity screen on Suite Three it must have been one of the inconspicuous mini-screens, and he didn't make it out. However, the door opened at his approach.

Inside, the large room looked more like living quarters than an office, which didn't surprise him. It was all the latest thing in the offices of high echelon executives. There was no desk.

A forty year old, give or take five years, stood up from a couch upon Brown's arrival and approached, hand extended.

"Please come in," he said pleasantly. "You are Mr. Brown, of course. My name is Francisco Byass."

He ushered Brown to a comfort chair. "Could I offer you a Sherry? We have our own cellars over in Jerez."

"No thank you," Brown said.

He took the other in. Senor Byass would not have been out of place in a similar office in London, Greater Washington, nor, Brown assumed, Moscow, for that matter. He was superlatively turned out, affable, well spoken and gave the impression of having all the time in the world to devote to Mr. Brown. There was but one thing. His eyes were empty.

Brown said, "I'll get to the point. I have heard that it is possible to secure just about anything in Satellite City. That it is the so-called sin-city of years past, brought to the ultimate. That any, uh, vice is available—given the price, of course."

Senor Byass had reseated himself on the couch. He smoothed his tiny mustache with a thumbnail and looked at his visitor calculatingly.

He said, "Mr. Brown, just about any vice that I can think of is available even here in Tangier since the Moroccan authorities have again made it an international city. Indeed, as the world is today, most of our vices are either old hat and seldom indulged, or are no longer considered vices. To what were you referring?"

Brown shrugged. "Narcotics, say?"

The other smiled in deprecation. "They are available,

Mr. Brown, but hardly profitable to organizations such as the Satellite City Authority. With modern medical means, there need no longer be withdrawal symptoms, and a cure of any addiction is possible within a matter of hours. You can smoke—marijuana, I believe you call it in your country—here in Tangier, or eat hashish for that matter. And when you had accomplished whatever it was you wished to accomplish, any doctor could treat you in such manner that you would have no after effects and, if you consulted either psychologist or psychiatrist afterward, you could be quickly cured of any desire to repeat your experiment as well."

He stook his head. "Dealing in narcotics is no longer profitable, Mr. Brown, certainly not in the advanced areas of the world, and it is only in such that there are sufficient resources to deal in *any* product profitably. For narcotics to be profitable, you must have a truly mass market. Marijuana, in the old days, did not appeal to organized . . . ah . . . endeavor, until literally millions began to smoke it. Opium, in the Orient, was profitable because, once again, millions were addicted to it and few were capable of being cured. But today? No, Mr. Brown, it is not worth bothering with. But I am sure that this is not your interest."

"No, of course not," Brown said, crossing his legs easily.

"Then, what is your interest?"

"Thrills," Brown said.

"I understand. There are quite a few available in Satellite City. Some, absolutely unavailable on Earth. What particular thrill, Mr. Brown?"

"Let me give you some background. I am of independent means and have been all my life in spite of present day all but confiscatory taxes. Since early youth, I have sought new thrills. Most of the sports, of course; mountain climbing, skin diving, racing cars and boats, big game fishing, flying gliders, stunting souped-up aircraft. All of the rest. I eventually found that the supreme thrill, for me at least, was in hunting, in killing, preferably the most dangerous game."

The other's eyebrows went up, slightly skeptical.

Brown said, a testiness in his voice, "Have you ever stalked a tiger in Bengal, Senor Byass, alone and armed only with a twenty-two pistol?"

The other was taken aback. "Why, of course not."

"Or an African lion, on one of the Kenya game perserves, for that matter?"

"No."

"Believe me, it can be quite thrilling."

"My dear Mr. Brown, there are no wild animals in space."

Brown ignored him. "I get my supreme thrill in killing, Byass, and fear that I have been born out of my time. In the past, when you lived to kill, you could always join an army currently involved in some war, or revolution, or whatever. Today, it has been a long time since we have had even what they used to call a bush war."

The eyes of Francisco Byass had narrowed.

Brown said easily, "I have killed, in my time, just about every animal worth bothering with—save a fellow human being."

II

For a long moment, Senor Byass took in his visitor. He found a man of about five foot ten, of about one sixty weight, and of possibly thirty years. There was a lazy quality, and the indolence extended to facial expression as well. An easy going face, fairly quick to make with a slight, somewhat rueful, smile. The eyes seemed to have a vulnerable quality. It was not a face that one would connect with a thrill seeker, an adventurer. But Senor Byass had long since learned that you cannot read character in a face. The most competent professional killer he had ever met had been fair of hair, baby blue of eye, all but cherubic facially and had been slightly effeminite; he had killed two police officers and wounded three more when finally brought to bay in circumstances under which the organization couldn't help him; indeed, under circumstances which the organization had instigated.

He said finally, "Mr. Brown, purely in the way of routine, what is your field of endeavor?"

"Ummm. I am an . . . investor."

"Of course. In, uh, what field?"

"In good things."

"Yes. And may I have the name of your Bank? This is all routine, of course."

"Of course. My major account is with the Grundbank in Geneva."

"I see. Under the name, Brown?"

12

"I have a numbered account."

"Of course. By the way, I might mention that banking facilities are even more, uh, far reaching, or shall we say discreet, in Satellite City."

"So I have heard. I intend looking into it."

"And now, before we go further. Would you please transfer one hundred thousand pseudo-dollars from your account to that of the Satellite City Authority?"

He who called himself Mr. Brown, hissed softly between his teeth. He said, "Just what will I buy with that sum?"

"Possibly nothing. In which case it will be returned to you. Possibly, when we have discussed it further, it will purchase what you wish, plus your passage to and from Satellite City and your accommodations and food while you are there."

Brown was obviously intrigued. "For how long a stay?"

"For as long as you wish."

"Suppose I wish to retire there?"

"Many have. Some for the sake of their health. There are many advantages in less gravity and sometimes free fall, for medical conditions. Or some remain because Satellite City has no extradition laws whatsoever, Mr. Brown. None whatsoever. For that matter, you might say it has no laws, in the usual sense."

"I'd think from your point of view there'd be a point of diminishing returns. Even a hundred thousand pseudo-dollars would be eaten up eventually."

"The Satellite City Orbital Resort Hotel provides quarters and meals, Mr. Brown, but there are other expenses. Your alcoholic beverages, or other escapes from reality, your gambling, your dallying with the fair sex—if that is your taste—your purchases in the shops. Oh, there

13

are quite a few things upon which to spend your funds in Satellite City. Believe me, we do not lose money on any guest who honors us."

"I suppose not." Mr. Brown brought his pocket phone cum identity card from an inner pocket and came to his feet. There was a phone screen on a small table at Byass' side. Brown turned it around to face him, and inserted the device in the screen's slot. He put his right thumb print on the identification square on the screen and said, "I wish to transfer one hundred . . ."

He broke it off and said to Byass, "Would you rather have it in pseudo-dollars or gold Swiss francs?"

The other said, "Either, or any other currency recognized on the world's bourses, for that matter."

Brown said into the screen. "I wish to transfer one hundred thousand pseudo-dollars to the account of the Satellite City Authority from my account with the Grundbank, Geneva, Switzerland."

The screen said, "Carried out."

Brown retrieved his pocket phone identity card and returned to his chair. "Okay. Great," he said. "And now what?"

"I assume that you do not wish any particular person. I am afraid that would be quite out of the question. If all you wished was for someone to be assassinated, you could have that arranged, at considerably less expense, in almost any metropolis in the world."

"No. I wish to do it myself, and I don't particularly care who it is."

Byass looked at him. "You say your hobby is hunting and that you have stalked Bengal tigers and lions armed with but a twenty-two pistol. It would be quite impossible, of course, for you to stalk your, uh, prey, through the corridors and public rooms of Satellite City."

"Of course." Brown allowed his tongue to run across a dry lower lip. "I am interested solely in the . . . kill."

"I see. It will take a bit of time to arrange."

"Understandable."

"Where can we get in touch with you?"

"I am staying at the New El Minzah."

. Bpass nodded. "Excellent choice. But this may take weeks."

"I'll remain in Morocco until you inform me that it's time to embark for Satellite City. There seem to be ample facilities for amusement here in Tangier."

"Yes. Ah, one last thing, Mr. Brown. Have you any preference in age, sex, or anything else? We go out of our way to give complete satisfaction."

Brown thought about it, even as he uncrossed his legs and stood. "I rather think a young and preferably pretty, and very expensively dressed, girl."

When he was gone, Senor Francisco Byass took a deep breath, exhaled and then shook his head. He touched a button and a younger man entered from another door.

Byass said, "You got photographs, Arturo?"

The newcomer couldn't have been older than the late twenties but already had an office pallor about him. He was obviously a flunky and had a mannerism of bobbing his head when answering a question.

He bobbed and said, "Yes, Senor Byass."

"Good enough to get the eye retinas?"

"Of course, Senor Byass."

"His thumbprint is now registered with the building's computer data banks. Check him out thoroughly. I want his complete dossier both from the International Data

Banks and the American National Data Banks. I also want his balance in the Geneva Grundbank. You'll best get in touch with Gritti, in Berne, for that. Gritti will be able to swing it—he'd better be able to."

"Yes, sir. Standard routine, of course, Senor Byass."

"That is correct, Arturo. One other thing. As soon as you have this, make an appointment for me to talk—scrambled, of course—with Mr. Rich in Satellite City."

The man who called himself Brown took the regular local jet over to the area once known as Algeria, and south to Colomb-Bechar. He was almost alone in the aircraft and spent his time staring down at the desolation which was the Sahara. It was not so bad nearest to the Mediterranean, where the reforestration which utilized the new desalinization processes was pushing back the desert which had been encroaching since the days of Carthage. He had little historical background but vaguely knew that the use of charcoal as a fuel, and the overgrazing of sheep and especially goats, had turned what once was the granary of the Roman Empire into useless wasteland.

At Columb-Bechar, the final outpost of civilization during the French regime, he stopped only long enough to get the still smaller shuttle helio-jet that was to take him down to Beni-Abbes and the spaceport there.

On that brief flight, he was able to look off to the left and to see the Grand Erg Occidental, the sand dunes once made famous by Hollywood in its highly fictional Foreign Legion films. Thus far, he had been moderately surprised to find that most of the Sahara was not composed of sand but rather of a hard gravel base.

Coming in for the landing at the spaceport, it took

only one sweeping look about the horizon to see why the area had been chosen for the purpose. The flatness stretched out in all directions for as far as the eye could range—even from the thousands of feet altitude from which they started down.

He had timed his arrival in such wise that he had only an hour to wait before the space transporter which was to take him up to Satellite City was ready for take-off.

He had seen photographs and even Tri-Di shows which involved the craft, many a time, but it still came as a moderate surprise to realize how very near an ordinary supersonic jet the craft looked, at this stage, at least. Wheels, wings, jet nacelles, the whole. However, he was knowledgeable enough to realize that at least half of this never left the stratosphere. Gone were the days when a multi-vehicle the size of a skyscraper was discarded, step by step, and allowed to be dropped back into the sea, or drift aimlessly in space, to launch a final module not much larger than a good sized closet.

He ascended the ramp to the passenger quarters and allowed one of the bustling stewardesses to strap him into his acceleration chair. There were evidently eight other passengers, one of whom sat immediately next to Brown and sounded off in a ceaseless chatter to the girl who was administering to him. His theme seemed largely to be how often he had made the hop, as he called it, and what an old spacehand he was. He wasn't as old as all that, possibly twenty-five.

Brown held his peace.

The stewardess who was taking care of him was a frisky little thing, most likely French, he decided. She chirped, "You went to the . . . bathroom, immediately before embarking, sir?"

"I didn't have to," Brown said.

"Are you thirsty? If you are thirsty, you had better let me get you a drink now."

"No," he said.

The garrulous one, next to him, grinned. "If you think you might need a crack at the bathroom, as she calls it, you'd better figure on it now, Jack. It's possible, but a lot of trouble, in free fall."

Brown said, "Thanks." He did not project himself as a warm man, and hardly the type to invite conversation from a stranger, but the other evidently hadn't the perception to realize that.

The passengers strapped in, all of the stewardesses, if that was the term, save one, left. She had a dozen or so final checks to make, including each of her charges and their strappings, then she too took her position in an acceperation chair, which evidently allowed for self-binding for the take-off. It occurred to Brown, only then, that he would find it very difficult releasing himself from his chair. In case of crack-up, while still Earth-bound, he wondered what provisions there were for passenger escape. And it came to him that there were possibly none, an uncomfortable feeling.

Forward, very similar to an ordinary passenger aircraft, there was a door, obviously leading to the crew's quarters of the spacecraft. A red light burned above it. It turned green and a sign lit up. *Take off of the Boostercraft.*

"Here we go," Brown's neighbor said, a note of satisfaction in his voice. Brown wondered how the man had reacted the first time he had made the flight. He had probably been in a sweat.

There was a small, tinted, very heavily glassed porthole next to him. Brown looked out. The take-off was no different than that of any of any other aircraft he had ever ridden. The quarters were more compact, the port-hole was considerably smaller and he felt like a papoose in its cocoon-like swathings, but otherwise he was still on home grounds.

It took them somewhat longer than usual to become airborne possibly, but otherwise everything was still the same.

"First trip, eh?" his neighbor said.

"That's right."

"Name's Cunningham. Franklin Cunningham. Frank. I work up in the City."

"Brown," Brown said. "Uh, Harold."

"Glad to meet you, Harry," the other told him. "Anything you want to know, just ask me. I been there and back so many times, I know the trail with my eyes closed." He laughed condescendingly.

He didn't wait for the questions, if Brown had any. He said, "They got this down pretty pat now. Pretty pat. Nothing to worry about. Back in the old days, you know how much fuel they had to burn just to get off the ground? Over two thousand tons. And then they just jettisoned that first stage. Threw it away. Must of cost millions. Just to barely get off the ground. You know how they do it now?"

Brown didn't have the time to answer, even if he had been inclined. The supersonic jet which was carrying them was zooming steeply for altitude.

"They take us up," Cunningham chuckled. "High as they can get us, going fast as they can go, see? And then our rockets start up, whoosh, and that's when you really begin to feel it. And, bang, they drop away, and go on back down. But, whoosh, we're just getting underway. You know why they do it that way?"

"Yes," Brown said. "I've read about it."

The other ignored him. "Because most of the expense in the blast-off used to be that first take-off, the first few feet off the ground. Now they get us up a lot of miles, maybe ten or twenty, I don't know, before we burn the first pound of rocket fuel, see? Then when we really get out into space, the nuclear power takes over. Hell, it's not much more expensive, the whole bit, than jet transportation. You know how high you're going?"

"Twenty-two thousand miles," Brown murmured.

"Twenty-two thousand miles," the other told him. "Just high enough so the City always sits there in the same place. Just stays there. I never been able to figure out why. Why it doesn't fall."

"For the same reason the moon doesn't," Brown said patiently.

"Yeah. That's what they say." The other chuckled again. "Hell, I never been able to figure why the moon doesn't fall."

The acceleration of their supersonic jet boostercraft was noticeable. Brown looked out his porthole at the rapidly receding surface of the desert below. He suspected that already he was as high as he had ever been. If his information was correct, the boostercraft was designed to go considerably higher than the usual transocean passenger and freight planes.

Beside him, young Cunningham was still chattering away in his self-assumed role as guide. Brown heard only a snatch of it. There were few people on Earth with even a meager education who didn't have a reasonably clear picture of the workings of Satellite City and how it was served.

"This is the longest part of the hop," Cunningham was saying. "Once we're on the rockets, the trip doesn't take any time at all. Unless the pilot louses up the docking. That can happen. That can happen."

Which was the only new item the other had come up with thus far. Just to say something, Brown said, "What then?"

"Nothing. He just has to make another pass. You know how it works, the docking?"

Before Brown could reply to that, the other gushed on. "This here Satellite City isn't just one satellite, you know. I don't even know how many there are, any more. I been on my Earth-side leave for three months. But there must of been maybe twenty, when I left. It's growing like crazy. Only three of them count. The big wheels, you know, like disks. They're about six hundred feet across and they turn, to give gravity, like. The orbital hotel, that's where you'll be going—you're not sick, ar you?"

"No," Brown said.

"The orbital hotel, it turns three revolutions a minute. That gives normal gravity on the rim. You know, centrifugal force, like. The rooms are built so your head is in the direction of the axis. You leave the rim rooms and start in the direction of the hub and the closer you get the more the gravity falls off. Same with the other big wheels. The orbital hospital has more of its rooms further in. Less gravity. Lot of the patients have things where it's better to have maybe half earth gravity. Some none at all." He laughed his forced, inane laugh. "Like if you had bedsores, imagine no gravity. But a lot of folks with heart trouble and stuff like that. Half gravity, or even quarter gravity, makes a lot of difference. You can do pretty well with a quarter gravity, almost normal walking and you don't have much to worry about the toilets and stuff like that."

The whoosh and bang described by Brown's unasked

informant had been surprisingly well described. Their space transport dropped away from the earthbound jet which had brought them to this altitude and the rockets cut in. The new acceleration pressed them back into their chairs.

The stewardess called out, cheerfully, "Everybody all right? We're under our own power now."

None of the passengers replied, and Brown suspected that his vocal companion was not the only repeat traveler to Satellite City. If there were others besides himself who were tyros to space they were evidently suffering no more than the sinking sensation he had in his own stomach. He hadn't expected hysteria. A person who would undertake the trip at all would hardly be the type to fall apart any more than aircraft passengers in the atmosphere on their first flight were inclined to more than initial nervousness.

Cunningham took up his monologue. "They've got to have this here dock because it'd be too much trouble for these transports to approach one of the wheels and match it's spin before it could zero-in. So the dock station don't spin. It just kind of sits there, off to one side of the big wheels and we dock there and then little shuttle craft, you don't need hardly any power at all for them, take you wherever you're going; to the orbital hotel, to the orbital hospital, or to the science wheel. You a scientist?"

"No," Brown said.

"Well, sir, there's a lot of these double-domes up here. Christ only knows what they're working on. I don't even know the names, like, of most of most of their sciences. Used to be you just had chemistry and biology and mathematics and a few like that. Now they got a million of them. Most of those guys don't even know what

22

they're talking about. They got these twenty-dollar words they pull on people trying to do the big impression razzle. They don't fool me. I always say, if what a guy says to me doesn't make any sense, it's probably because there's no sense to it. If you can't understand what he's talking about, he probably don't either. That's what I say."

Brown wished that the porthole was larger. He had many times seen photographs, TV and Tri-Di shots of the Earth from space, and of Luna and the satellites, including Satellite City, from space, but to witness it was fascinating.

Cunningham was saying, "The hydroponics wheel spins just a little bit. About a quarter earth gravity on the rim. You heard about the hydroponics?"

"Yes, I have," Brown said.

"Well, you'd be surprised. When they first started this Satellite City, way back before they called it that, they had to ship up everything, see? And that was before they had these transporters down so pat. They had to send up even air and water, not to talk about food. Now you know how much of our own stuff we make?"

"No, I suppose not," Brown said.

"Ninety, maybe ninety-five percent. You got no idea how stuff grows with no gravity, or precious little. I've seen corn on the cob so big one kernel is enough for what you'd ordinarily eat. Damn good, too. And you oughta see the fruit. Just this last few years they been raising chickens and pigs, too. And they got this new deal for raising beef. You ever heard of Kobe beef?"

"Yes," Brown said.

"Well, what Kobe beef is, the Japanese started it a long time ago. They never let the steer out of his stall. No exercise, see? The farmers that raise them, whenever one of the family has a few minutes time off their other work, they'd go out and massage this steer. And they'd feed him the best. Used to give him beer to drink. Anyway it was the tenderest beef in the world. And that's what they're experimenting with up here now, only, of course, the massaging and all is automated. And another thing. You know what? At first, they didn't even have the chickens. We just raised our own vegetables and fruit and they give off the oxygen we need, see? But they found out that animal fertilizer helped in this kind of closed circuit way of making the food. Like the animals breathe in oxygen and they breathe out whatever it is you breathe out and the plants need that. And they eat some of the plants and . . ." he laughed inanely ". . . the manure, it goes back to the plants. And all the garbage from the big wheels, where we live, it goes back to the hydroponic wheel and they grind it up, or whatever they do, and it goes back to feed the plants too. Nothing is wasted."

Brown sucked in air. "Look, friend," he said. "I think I'll take a little nap."

The other was only slightly miffed. "Go on ahead," he said. "But it won't be long before you can see Satellite City. It's pretty, the first time you see it."

III

He sat with his eyes closed to simulate sleep but couldn't keep himself from wondering about the other. If he had it correctly, Cunningham was permanently employed in Satellite City. Why, after, supposedly, years of experience in the place hadn't he even informed himself on why a satellite, twenty-two thousand miles above the earth's surface, kept from falling. Perhaps he was one of those who shoveled the animal manure, chicken, hog and steer, from the animal stalls to the hydroponic tanks. But no, that didn't make sense. Obviously, all that would be automated, as well as the cleaning of stalls and so forth.

He was irritated with himself to be thinking about Cunningham at all. He had other things on his mind. In fact, he was having second thoughts about this whole venture. In spite of the affability of Byass and all others he had met connected with the Satellite City Authority, they were obviously very competent citizens indeed. And, no question about it, once he had blown free of earth, they had him in their power. Also, they had no motivation whatsoever, as an organization, except the acquisition of wealth—and they knew he had wealth.

His neighbor was evidently able to restrain himself from displaying his superior knowledge on matters pertaining to Satellite City. But only temporarily. Brown received a nudge in the side.

"Hey, Harry," Cunningham said. "We're coming in.

Look out there, kind of forward, you can see one of the tanks."

Brown sighed and opened his eyes. "What tanks?"

"I was telling you about all the little satellites, besides the big wheels. They're mostly storage. Or some of them are empty, waiting to be joined up. This thing is growing like crazy. You think this whole transporter we're in is just going to go on back to Beni-Abbes and pick up another load? Hell no. All that goes back is this front end, like. Where the crew is and the passenger quarters. The rest, it gets emptied out of all the stuff we're carrying and the shell it gets welded on to the orbital hotel, or wherever. No use sending it all the way up here and then letting it go back empty. These things don't just carry passengers. They carry everything, freight and all, then they get welded on. Or maybe they're designed to be storage tanks. For fuel and things like that. They got it all down pat."

"I've read about it," Brown said wearily. He could have cut the other down to size, shut him up, but he didn't want to draw unusual attention to himself. So far as he was concerned, he hoped that no one with whom he came in contact would remember him. His purpose in coming to Satellite City wasn't exactly one in which you wished to be conspicuous.

Cunningham was saying, "You'd be surprised how this place is growing. I don't know anybody ever figured it'd get this big. The orbital hotel. You know how big it was first? Only one level, one floor. And a lot of space between the rim and the axis wasn't anything but girders. Now it'll go up as many as six floors. They got some people with permanent suites. Spend half the year up here. Hell, some of them especially those with heart conditions, they spend *all* their time up here. Afraid to go on back to earth gravity. They get themselves an apartment, maybe halfway between the rim and the axis, about half gravity, see? Then they just live there. Man, don't think that doesn't run into expense."

Through the porthole, Brown could see several of the free floating tanks, the oddly shaped containers. Obviously, steamlining meant nothing in space. On some of them, he could make out tiny figures in spacesuits, obviously working at joining different elements. He hadn't realized, in spite of his reading, that the project was of this magnitude. Although transport costs had been minimized, compared to the old days, this thing must run into billions. Of course, most of that expense, decades ago, had been borne by the earth governments and particularly his own. He wondered at what political pull, what graft, had gone into turning it over to a private corporation.

A sign above the entrance to the crew's compartment lit up. It said, simply, *Docking*.

His neighbor chuckled. "Now we'll dock it," and his tone suggested that he, himself, was somehow involved with the operation.

Brown could feel slight changes in course, this way, that way, gently, as the pilot evidently jockeyed his craft into the space dock. Then there was a clanging and a feeling of halt of motion, although, of course, he was perfectly aware of the fact that the whole conglomerate which was Satellite City was speeding through space at a velocity of thousands of miles an hour.

Their stewardess unbuckled herself from her chair, with a few flicks of her hands, and, with obvious expertise in free fall, pulled herself over to the hatchway and dropped a lever.

A swarm of dock workers entered, also working in free fall, also obviously well used to the condition. They were all coverall clothed, lettering on their backs reading, *Satellite City,* and a patch over each left breast giving their names.

One was evidently an officer and carried an official looking list in his hands.

"Please respond to your names," he called out, and began to read.

"Franklin Chichak."

A middle aged man said, "Here."

Two of the coveralled workers approached his acceleration chair and did things to it.

The officer said, "Hospital," and the two workers jockeyed the chair from the compartment. Brown couldn't quite see if it was on wheels or not. Possibly wheels weren't necessary.

His name was last.

"Harold Brown."

"That's me."

"Orbital hotel," the officer said, and Brown's chair in turn was jockeyed out of the hatch.

Five of the other passengers were also scheduled for the hotel. All were pushed down a rather bleak corridor, so narrow as to admit of only one chair at a time, and to a new and considerably smaller shuttlecraft which they entered through what Brown decided was undoubtedly some sort of air lock. The attendents made their acceleration chairs secure to the floor again and, in no more than minutes, had closed the hatch behind them.

The officer with the list of their names had accompanied them. He said, his voice easy, and with calming tone, "I note that this isn't a first visit for most of you. We are, of course, simply shuttling over to the hotel. We are now in free fall, so it isn't practical to release you from your chairs. Once on the wheel, you'll find everything surprisingly Earth-side."

Nobody said anything.

Shortly they could feel movement of the shuttlecraft and within a few moments, metalic sounds of docking again. It was all very efficiently done.

When the hatch opened this time, a new swarm of attendents entered, including young women. Each passenger had one girl, very trimly uniformed, her name sewn over her left breast in letters of gold, and one maroon uniformed male helper who devoted himself to the acceleration chair's bindings.

In short order, they were all emerging into the reception hall, or whatever it might be termed. There were various others there to greet them, some obviously Satellite City employees, some friends or business associates of the new arrivals. For the first time since they had left Earth, a sizeable amount of chatter broke out. It just came to Brown now how remarkably quiet they had all been, save Cunningham, for the duration of the space flight. He decided it was because there was something awesome about space, even for those who had made the journey before.

There was a very minimal amount of checking of papers and polite directions or questions on the part of the Satellite City employees.

Brown's girl said brightly, "Mr. Brown? I'll see you to your quarters. Your luggage has already been delivered."

"Fine," he told her. She was, as most of these employees seemed to be, bright and brisk; the airline stewardess type, only upgraded a few points in both efficiency and attractiveness. The job must really be considered desirable, Brown decided.

She began to lead the way but one of the uniformed attendants whose outfit differed slightly from those of the others, perhaps being less colorful, came up.

"Mr. Brown," he said politely, "would you mind coming this way for just a moment?"

His girl looked slightly surprised, blinked and remained where she was. Brown, inwardly shrugging, followed the other to a door which read, in small letters, simply *Protective*.

The door opened before them, though seemingly there was no identity screen.

There were other doors that led beyond, but the immediate office into which Brown was ushered was neat, comfortable and very *polite*. There was one desk and the young man seated behind it was conservatively uniformed, as friendly of expression as a bank officer initially meeting a multi-millionaire who was a potential new client, and was obviously a gentleman. And he had very cold eyes.

He came to his feet, rounded the desk and shook hands with Brown in exactly the correct manner. Everything he did was exactly correct, Brown was to find.

He said, "Mr. Brown, welcome to Satellite City. We sincerely desire that your stay here be most enjoyable. My name is Berch, Antony Berch. I certainly hope I can serve you while you are with us."

"Thank you," Brown said.

The other, frowning very slightly, perched himself on the corner of his desk, leaning on one hip.

He said, as though distressed, "Mr. Brown, this is, we understand, your first visit to Satellite City."

"Yes."

"Unfortunately, though we refrain from interfering

with our guests to every extent possible, we have a few regulations."

"I'm sure you have."

The other said carefully, "One of our regulations, Mr. Brown, is that no guest, nor anyone else for that matter, is allowed possession of firearms while in Satellite City. I am sorry."

"I see," Brown said. He brought the gyro-jet pistol from the holster under his left arm and placed in on the desk. He said, "I suppose I am a bit romantic, but I'd heard about Tangier and brought this along for self-protection."

Antony Berch was most understanding. "Of course, sir. We shall keep this in our custody until you leave."

"Of course," Brown repeated.

The young man who had ushered him to this office, cleared his throat. He said, "The scanner indicated further ... metal, Mr. Berch."

The Protective officer, as they evidently liked to call themselves, looked at Brown.

Harold Brown frowned puzzlement and shook his head.

The two Satellite City men held their peace but kept their eyes upon him expectantly.

He put his hands in his pockets, scowling lack of understanding, and brought forth several of the usual items men carry. One was a somewhat oversized pocketknife.

Berch said, "Fred?"

The junior officer took the knife and looked at it. "Swiss," he said. "The kind boy scouts carry."

There were half a dozen blades. One was a nail file, one a cork screw, one a punch, one a small blade, and one a two incher. There was even a screwdriver.

31

Fred cleared his throat again and handed it back. "Sorry, sir," he said.

"Not at all," Brown told him. His smile was wry. "I've carried it since boyhood. I don't know why, any longer." And to Antony Berch, "Is that all?"

"Of course. Sorry to be so discourteous, Mr. Brown. Once again, I sincerely hope you find your stay enjoyable."

"I'm sure I will," Brown said. He turned and followed the younger officer from the room.

His girl, her expression slightly concerned, was awaiting him. His reappearance evidently reassured her. Brown wondered vaguely to just what extent the so-called Protective officers could possibly go. As he understood it, the Satellite City Authority was a law unto itself. No earth nation, no earth body even such as the Reunited Nations, had jurisdiction here in space. Nevertheless, he couldn't imagine such institutions as a local prison, though, come to think of it, why not? What happened in the unlikely case that some resident, or employee, robbed another? He had never read of a court of law in Satellite City and now that he thought about it, that was on the strange side. It occurred to him that any news, any internal development, anything period that emanated from Satellite City was filtered through its own organization before ever appearing on the news, or in any publication on the surface of Earth. And once again it now occurred to him, that he had never read anything derogative about Satellite City and its administration. Everything, but everything, was just absolutely tip-top with never a gear lacking adequate grease in all ramifications of Satellite City affairs.

He followed her down an ornately done corridor, admiring the gentle sway of her generous hips, while she chattered briskly. "For your first few days, at least, Mr. Brown, you will be quartered right here on the rim. Gravity is exactly Earth-side, so you have no problem whatsoever in acclimating yourself. Later on, if you wish, and you most likely will, you can change your suite to one a bit further in toward the axis and have the interesting experience of three quarters, or even one half or one quarter Earth-side gravity. It can be a lot of fun."

"I would imagine it could be interesting," Brown said.

"Oh yes." She looked at him from the side of her eyes, very perkily. "One warning, sir."

"Oh?"

"For some reason, lesser gravity has somewhat the same effect as being at high altitude Earth-side. Alcohol seems to have a greater influence. Three quarters gravity gives quite an additional . . ." she tinkled a laugh ". . . lift. Half gravity is absolutely bouncy if you're a bit . . ." she tinkled again ". . . high. And a quarter gravity, or free fall, is out of this world."

He realized that it was probably a standard little gag she delivered to every newcomer in her charge.

"I'm not much of a drinker," he told her.

She came to what was evidently his door, Suite K-1, and it opened at their approach. He had expected accommodations in Satellite City to be somewhat on the austere side, and possibly they had been only a decade or so before, but seemingly time was marching on with a vengence. The door had an identity screen and it had already been keyed to his individuality.

Austere, no, but it was still obvious that Satellite City took cognisance of space and the expense of ferrying furniture and luxury appointments twenty-two thousand miles straight up. It was well done, very well done; but you were in a suite in Satellite City, not in a luxury hotel of Birritz, the Crimea, Neuve Acapulco, or Antarctica-town. It was a bit difficult to put your finger upon. Nothing as obvious as steel walls or floor; nevertheless, in spite of the clever interior decorating, which achieved a feeling of spaciousness, he knew that if he reached a hand up he could touch the ceiling. He knew very well that the carpeting was such that an elephant stampede would not have resulted in signs of wear. And although it was named a suite, the three rooms were such that had he been even a trifle on the larger side he wouldn't have had too much trouble standing in the middle of the bathroom and touching the walls to both sides.

He looked about and said, "A bit small, isn't it?"

She said very quickly, "We have larger suites, Mr. Brown. They are a bit more——"

He said, "Price is of no moment. However, this will be adequate for the first day or two, at least. As you say, I'll have to become acclimated."

"Certainly, sir. Your baggage is in the bedroom, Mr. Brown. A valet is available if you wish. Your order screen, there on the table, is exactly the same as Earthside. If you wish additional clothing, or refreshments, or anything else . . ."

She let the sentence dribble away and stood there for a moment, as though awaiting questions.

He said, "Thank you. I'll do fine."

She said, indicating the small desk, "There is a little directory, telling you about the orbital hotel's facilities, giving diagrams and a complete map of the areas open to the guests, and a list of all departments you might wish to call upon. If you wish, a guide will be here immediately.

"Not for the time."

She was being perky again and eyed him from the

34

sides of her eyes. "If you need . . . me, for anything, I'm available."

That set him back a little. It had never occurred to him. Well . . . he could imagine. At a hundred thousand a throw, and that just a preliminary, before other expenses, anything, but anything, should be available.

He said, "Thanks. Possibly I'll call on you later."

She seemed slightly disappointed. "My name's Gertrude," she said, "And my department is Service."

When she was gone, he looked at the door, after her. "I'll bet it is," he said meaninglessly.

IV

He spent possibly half an hour exploring the small suite, unpacking, figuring out the workings of his new quarters. In the living room he found two simulated windows, very cleverly done so that what were actually tridi photographs, partly animated, seemingly looked out upon ordinary earth scenes. One portrayed a valley, complete with a quiet lake, the other, a mountain scene, probably the Alps, with considerable depth. He suspected that there might be, in some visitors to Satellite City, a tendency toward claustrophobia. The pseudo-windows would go far to help.

He found also a true window behind a sliding panel in the floor and activated by a button. The glass, assuming it was glass rather than some new development resultant of space technology, was similar to that in his porthole in the space transporter; obviously very thick and tinted. Through it, he could look out into space. However, the speed of rotation of the orbit hotel wheel was on the disconcerting side. What had that kid Cunningham said? The wheel turned three times a minute to maintain normal gravity on the rim. A construction six hundred feet in diameter was going at a goodly clip to rotate three times a minute. He closed the panel, blocking out space. Possibly he could get used to it later. Further in, of course, if he changed his quarters, the speed would be less. Or, if he went to the axis and experienced the free fall there—something he wanted to try, before he left—there would be no sense of turning at all, so he assumed.

His immediate chores and explorations over, he had a feeling of *what now?* He sat down at the small desk and looked into the pamphlet of hotel offerings and the charts of the corridors and public rooms. He was moderately surprised. There were four restaurants in all, several bars and night spots of varying size, a swimming pool, three gyms, in different degrees of gravity, and three gambling rooms, evidently one large casino and two more intimate ones for card games. There was also a largish room called the Bourse—stock market exchange, to him. Two theatres provided additional entertainment, although his quarters contained the usual large screened Tri-De set which was undoubtedly hooked up to the amusement data banks on earth, so that he could select any production either current or of the past right here in his living room. Possibly the theatres were for living productions. He could imagine that ballet, for instance, might have ramifications in half gravity, not to speak of free fall.

There was an autobar set into one corner and he had about decided to try a drink, in spite of—what was her name?—Gertrude's warning, when the identity screen on the door buzzed. He looked over at it. There was the face of a complete stranger. A cheerful enough face, but an unknown.

He went on over and opened up.

The newcomer wore civilian dress, was possibly in his early thirties, and seemed a bit less brisk than most that Brown had met in his Satellite City associations thus far.

Brown looked at him questioningly.

The other grinned and said, "Ericsson. Scoop Ericsson. Public relations."

"I don't need any," Brown said flatly.

The other nodded. "That's what I came to see you about."

Brown stood aside and closed the door after the other when he had entered.

The newcomer said, "Mind if I sit down?"

"Of course not. Drink?"

The other grinned again. He was evidently a smiling type. Brown had come to the conclusion, long since, that a smiling type man did not necessarily have a great deal of humor in his make-up.

"I've been a newsman ever since I got out of school. In that time, I've never met a colleague who didn't drink, with the exception of a few who belonged to A.A. I'm not quite ready for Alcoholics Annonymous . . . yet." Evidently, this particular smiling type man did have some humor.

Brown went over to the bar. "What does one drink in Satellite City? I've been warned that the stuff gets to you in free fall."

"It does, but here on the rim you're not in free fall, so it's all about the same. You drink anything you want . . . anything. If you're watching your pennies, like we employees have to, you drink one of the spirits such as gin or vodka, or whiskey or rum. If you're loaded like most of the guests—hell, like all of the guests—you drink anything from stone age Metaxa to vintage champagne. The bars even stock absinthe."

Brown looked at him from the bar. "Why should gin and the other spirits be any cheaper?"

"Because we make it up here. Alcohol's no problem in the hydroponic compartments. Gin and vodka are just is alcohol with a little flavoring added. Whiskey and rum too, for that matter, though they need a bit more finesse. Actually, the laboratory boys have long since dreamed up ways of making better booze than used to come out of the highly advertised distilleries in the old days. But they can't duplicate vintage champagne or some of the other fancy liquors."

"I see," Brown said. "Well, what'll it be?"

"Gin and tonic's okay with me."

Brown flicked on the autobar and said into the screen, "Two gin and tonics, please."

When they had come, he carried one over to the publicity man, then found a chair for himself, made the gesture of toast and said, "First one today with this hand."

The other nodded and took an appreciative sip.

Brown said, "Scoop?"

The other grinned in self-deprecation. "Kind of a gag name the boys hung on me while I was still a gung-ho kid. In the old days, the public used to think that newsmen called an exclusive news break a scoop. They didn't. They called it a beat, but there was no use telling the public that, they knew darned well it was a scoop and a scoop it had to be in fiction or films, or whatever."

Brown said flatly, "I don't want any publicity about my coming to Satellite City. In fact, I don't like the fact that you've shown up at all."

Ericsson nodded reassuringly. "That's why I'm here to see you. Possibly three quarters of the folks who come up here feel the same way. And they get exactly what they want. Not even so much as a single mention anywhere in the world's news media, that they've come to Satellite City. Not only do we not release it, but we twist the arms of any others who try to deal with Satellite City affairs. More than one reporter, down Earth-side, has been bounced off his job because he didn't take a gentle hint. Some of our people in the Satellite City Authority throw a lot of weight."

He shrugged and took another sip of his gin and tonic. "On the other hand, sometimes you get these playboy types who like to see their faces on the news screens. Like to show off that they have the admittedly king-size funds to blow on a live-it-up trip to Satellite City. Or sometimes we get well heeled honeymooners. We give them all the coverage in the world—always making certain, of course, that there is nobody in the background that might be picked up by the lens, who doesn't want publicity."

Brown was interested. "But what if some newshawk, not connected with your organization, comes to Satellite City with the idea of doing a bang-up, uh, sin-city type story?"

"In the first place, darn few could afford it. In the second place, we'll sell passage to darn few who can. In the third, before we sell them passage we get a written statement not to write about it unless we clear all copy. You'd be surprised how difficult it is to get practically *any* copy past my desk, Mr. Brown. Oh, we're not so tough in the orbital hospital and especially the science wheel, but here in the hotel?" The newsman shook his head definitely. "Practically impossible to write anything more revealing than what's on the menu in the Asiatic Dining Room."

"But suppose one of them breaks his promise?"

Ericsson grinned. "Ha! We land on him like a load of bricks. We have the written statement not to print anything we haven't cleared. We sue. No matter if what they write is up-beat, we still sue. We sue the reporter and we sue his editor and we sue the publisher. We sue everybody in sight."

Brown was intrigued now. "Have you ever had to sue anyone?"

"Only once. A Swede. He thought he was going to run an expose series, under a different name. Most of it he'd made up out of the whole cloth. It never came to trial. The poor guy had an accident a couple of weeks before the trial was scheduled. We contacted the publisher and had the story suppressed."

Brown looked at him. "What kind of an accident?"

"Just an accident. Manually driving an electro-steamer up in the mountains. Some larger vehicle must've come along and crowded him off over a cliff."

The publicity man had finished his drink. He stood. "Okay," he said. "No publicity whatsoever. In fact, Mr. . . . Mr. . . . ah . . ." he grinned. "See? I've just forgotten your name. Enjoy your stay in Satellite City. You'll find privacy such as you've never known before. The Authority makes a fetish of it. To my knowledge there is not a single bug in the whole orbital hotel. No phone calls are recorded. The identity screens in the elevators and so forth make no reports to the computer data banks of your comings and goings. The guests like it that way, and that's what they get."

Brown said, "Wait a minute. Have another. This is my first couple of hours here. I'd like to ask some questions."

The other cocked his head. "Sure. Just so it doesn't involve any other guests."

Brown got up for a fresh drink for the other, although he had barely touched his own. Settled down again, he said, "Like everybody, I've been reading about Satellite City since I was a kid. Since it was hardly more than

41

started. But I had no idea of the magnitude of the thing. Why, it must involve billions of pseudo-dollars."

Ericsson nodded, just a bit warily. "I wouldn't know the exact amount, of course, it's not my business, but I assume the computers have it all figured out to the last penny, somewhere or other. However, it's a big operation, all right."

"Well, what gets me is the source of income. Sure, they charge the highest hotel rates ever known, but . . . well . . . it's still peanuts."

The other nodded and had obviously gone into this before. He said, "Mr. Brown, you might call this the final stand of *laissez faire* classical capitalism. The culmination of free enterprise. This is Wall Street, the City of London, Switzerland and the old International Zone of Tangier, all wrapped into one, and with goodies added."

Brown scowled. "I'm not sure I follow you."

The other snorted deprecation. "You're not exactly poor, Mr. Brown, or you wouldn't be here. Let's put it this way. In the world economy, and especially in the developed countries, the post-industrial part of the world, everything is in a condition of flux. They call the socio-economic system by various names; Meritocracy, the New Industrial State, People's Capitalism, the Welfare State, State Capitalism. The Soviet Complex still pretends they've got a form of Communism. Ha! But at any rate, to keep these economies going, they've got to tax everything that will stand still long enough to be taxed, from chewing gum to cosmocorps the size of International Communications, not to speak of individual incomes and fortunes. The loopholes they used to have have been plugged up with a determination grand to behold. Oil depletion, farm subsidies, foundations, trusts, ways of ducking inheritance taxes—ha! They get them all, now."

"You tell me little," Brown said sarcastically. "My lawyer's bill costs me a fortune yearly."

"Ummm. But let's take a look at Satellite City. The Swiss used to think they had some free-wheeling banking laws what with their numbered accounts and so forth. Ha!—once again. Let me give you an example. Suppose you have a hundred million to invest. You put it into one of the big Earth-side corporations, that hasn't so far been assimilated by some government, and because you're lucky, or in the know, the stock doubles in value. So you sell. Swell. They nick you fifty percent—it used to be only twenty-five—for capital gains. If you don't sell, and take your profit, they nick you ninety percent or so income tax on the dividends that you get."

Ericsson grinned and took another pull at his drink. "Sometimes I'm glad I'm no multi-millionaire."

"But here in Satellite City?" Brown prodded.

"On the Bourse, here, there is no record, Earth-side, of the exchanges that take place. You bank your hundred million in the Satellite City Authority Bank and invest it in, say, some of the new Japanese submarine freighter shipyards. The stock booms. You take your profit. And the only tax here is five percent capital gains. Five percent, instead of fifty. That's also the income tax on dividends on any securities you hold here in Satellite City."

Brown puckered his lips. "It doesn't sound like much."

"I've heard rumors of deals here that involved up to one billion pseudo-dollars in profits, Mr. Brown. Do you know what five percent of a billion pseudo-dollars mounts up to?"

"Obviously."

The newsman said dryly, "Satellite City is not exactly going broke. And the Bourse is only one source of income. Possibly the largest, but only one. The orbital hotel operation, the orbital hospital, wealthy people who retire here, to avoid taxes, or for their health, or whatever else. Oh, there are other things too. Some of the science breakthroughs that have been made. The teams that make them are well enough paid, wonderfully paid, but most of these double-domes aren't particularly interested in money. They're hot to have the equipment, the circumstances here under which they can work at their disposal. And what happens to the rights on the discoveries they make? Usually they're assigned to the Satellite City Authority. Oh, they're a lot of profitable little items up here, Mr. Brown."

He finished his drink and came to his feet again. "If there's anything at all my department can help you on, all you have to do is call."

Brown stood too and saw the other to the door. "I doubt if there will be." He added, flatly, "And any publicity shots you might be taking, be sure I'm not in the background . . . Scoop."

The other grinned. "Of course."

V

It occurred to Brown that he hadn't eaten since the light lunch he had taken on the jet between Tangier and Columb-Bechar.

He went over to the phone screen on the desk and activated it, "Time, please."

A pretty girl's face was in the screen. It came to him that all of the girls he had thus far seen in Satellite City would be candidates for beauty contests back on Earth and thus far he doubted if any of them had been above thirty in age.

This one said, "We keep Prime Meridian hours in Satellite City, Mr. Brown. It is now 20 hours and 23 minutes, Greenwich time. However, we can give you the time for any location Earth-side, if you wish."

Brown thanked her, flicked the screen off and looked at his watch. He had reset it, at the stewardess' suggestion, over Algeria, and evidently Columb-Bechar had also been in the same zone as the Prime Meridian. No wonder he was hungry, it was almost half past eight.

He looked at the table set against one wall. A servotable, which could seat four. He considered eating right here in his quarters. However, he was curious about the public rooms and decided to look up the restaurants in the directory. They were cosmopolitan to say the least. He decided upon the Galaxy Room, the largest, worked out the route to take to it and was about to leave when something else came to him.

He flicked on the desk screen again and said, "Is evening wear required in the restaurants?"

The girl said, "Only in the Galaxy Room, sir. Oriental garb is usual in the Asiatic Room but is not required, particularly of Caucasians."

Brown said, "In view of the baggage limitations, I failed to bring evening clothes."

She said, "Sir, if you will just stand before the mirror in your bath and order . . ."

That was a new one to him. He went into the btth. The mirror was full length and, yes, there was a phone screen above it.

He stood there and said, "I would like evening clothes, complete to shoes."

The screen thanked him. "They will be in your closet, sir."

"How soon? I'm in a bit of a hurry."

"Immediately, sir."

He grunted at that and made his way to his bedroom. Sure enough, the suit was there. So were shirt, underclothing, tie, cummerbund, socks and shoes.

Interested, he took the suit down and looked at it with close care. Seemingly, it was brand new. However, on a suspicion he examined it very closely. It would have set him back at least a couple of hundred pseudo-dollars in London's Bond Street.

He was mildly amused. The garments had been touched up with considerable art but the suit was not truly new. Evidently, the services here in Satellite City weren't above making a quick pseudo-dollar from every source possible. A guest would come up from Earth, his wardrobe limited, and find evening wear de rigueur. He would buy what was required, probably at some astronomical price, and then, upon leaving, discard the expensive clothing, worn only a few times at most, which would be carefully refurbished and be sold again to the next guest of that exact size. Satellite City might be rolling in wealth but its orbital hotel, like every hotel on earth, watched each penny with a miser's eye.

He shucked off his jacket and worked out of the holster rig which had nestled his gyro-jet gun under his left arm. He tossed the rig into a dresser drawer, ruefully. He might have known that they'd have some sort of scanner in the reception hall of the hotel. Satellite City could afford no scandal; they'd be very careful of such items as violence between guests, or even suicide. He wondered how lengthy the longer blade of his knife would have had to have been before they would have confiscated that as well.

He dressed, finding the suit a perfect fit, but ignored the cummerbund. He had never liked the things, even though they were currently in fashion.

He returned to the living room and looked at the autobar, wondering whether or not to have a quick one before heading for the restaurant. He shook his head. Thus far, he was up in the air on what was to develop, but if there was anything he wanted to be sure of, it was clarity, and he had already had one drink.

He turned to the door but at that moment the identity screen buzzed and a stranger's face was there.

He opened up and raised eyebrows. There were two newcomers. The one whose face had been in the screen was a very well done up, very suave type of about forty. Brown was reminded of Senor Byass, back in Tangier; even to the empty eyes, it seemed. They might have been brothers.

Brown said, "Yes?"

"My name is Rich, Mr. Brown. Al Rich. I am of the Satellite City Authority staff."

Brown stood back. "Come in."

The two entered. The second was a younger man, a little on the heavy-set side and though presentably turned out was obviously not the gentleman Rich projected himself as being. He had the mannerism of looking away from the face of those with whom he was in contact, not just the eyes, but the face. His own dark eyes would go from his feet, to a picture on the wall, to the desk, to a chair, continually in movement, but never to a face, even though he was talking to someone. Rich didn't bother to introduce him.

Brown said, "What can I do for you?"

"I've been assigned to . . . handle your requirements, Mr. Brown," the other said carefully.

Brown's eyes went to the younger of the two. He said, "I'd like as few persons as possible to be privy to the matter, Mr. Rich."

"Of course." The staff man turned to his companion. "Stay out in the hall, Rocky."

Rocky nodded silently, took in Brown from his neck down to his shoes, turned and moved easily through the door. He had a smooth grace somewhat inconsistent with his build. He shut the door behind him.

Rich said, "I see you are about to go out. For dinner, undoubtedly. I won't take too much of your time."

Brown looked at him questioningly, waiting for him to go on.

"You are still interested in going through with your . . . project?"

"Why not? I paid the rather ridiculously high fee."

"Of course. I simply dropped by to make sure."

"Okay. Great."

Al Rich said, his voice suave, "It was thought that perhaps on reflection, you might change your mind."

"Why?"

The newcomer shrugged. "You never know. At any rate, our suggestion is that you take a preliminary twenty-four hours here in Satellite City. I assure you they will not be boring. If you still wish to go through with it, we are at your service."

"Very well," Brown said.

The staff man turned back to the door. "Were you planning to dine in the Galaxy Room?"

"Why, yes."

"I'm going there. I'll escort you, if you wish."

"Thanks."

In the corridor, outside, the silent, shifty-eyed Rocky fell in step behind them.

Al Rich said, "And what are your impressions of our Satellite City, thus far, Mr. Brown?"

"I haven't been here long enough to have a good many, but thus far I'm impressed by the efficiency."

The other nodded. "We try."

"And also by the extent to which you've been able to so duplicate Earth-side—that's the term you use, isn't it?"

"Yes, Earth-side."

"The extent to which you've been able to duplicate conditions there. You have to keep reminding yourself that you're over twenty-thousand miles away from home."

"This is home to a good many, Mr. Brown. For health, and other reasons. You'd be surprised how many full time retirees we have."

"Oh? I can see why some would chose to live here,

heart conditions, and so forth, but who else . . . ?"

The other looked at him from the side of his eyes. He said, "We take the elevator here," stopping before it. "The Galaxy Room is one floor up, or rather *in* to be accurate."

"Oh? Then the gravity will be less?"

"Not noticibly, with only one floor involved."

They stepped into the elevator and the silent Rocky joined them. Rich spoke softly into the screen and the elevator mounted.

"As to your question, various of our guests find it more, ah, expedient, or let us say politic, to remain here, free of the world's, ah, caprice. For instance, a month or so ago it became necessary for us to join several compartments in order to construct a suitable suite for our latest permanent guest and his harem. The Sheik Abd el Suliman condescended to honor us. A direct descendent of the Prophet, you know. It seems that as chief of his tribe the oil revenues accruing to the sheikdom were all rendered into his name. Realizing that his people would not appreciate roads, hospitals, schools and such effeminacies of the West, he transferred the oil royalties to the Satellite City Authority Bank. Some of his people took exception to his decision, and he felt it best to retire here, free from the threats of disgruntled malcontents."

"I see. I suppose it would be difficult for any of them to up here."

They reached the next floor and stepped from the elevator directly into as well done a restaurant as Brown could ever remember having seen. The *maitre d'* approached them, beaming.

"Very difficult," Al Rich said, nodding. "We also have a few retired political figures, particularly from the Latin

American countries. The former treasurer of the Caribbean League, for instance." He wound it up. "You might keep it in mind, Mr. Brown. In this age, one never knows when one might decide to, ah, end one's years in quiet seclusion in a resort which has available all of the amenities to be found anywhere else—and even a few facilities most difficult to come by elsewhere. As you are already aware."

He turned to the hovering *maitre d'* and said, "Warren, Mr. Brown is a new guest. Be sure the chefs outdo themselves."

Warren bowed, just the exact number of inches appropriate. "You are alone, Monsieur Brown?"

"Yes," Brown said. He said to Rich, "I assume I'll be seeing you later."

"In twenty-four hours, if not before, my dear Mr. Brown."

Brown followed the head waiter to his table.

That worthy cleared his throat gently and said, "It occurs to me, Monsieur, that perhaps a table companion would be desirable. Only a few moments ago, another guest honored us with her presence. A very attractive young lady who seems somewhat . . . lonesome."

"Oh?" Brown said, as the other helped seat him at a table for two.

"If Monsieur will look slightly to the right. There in the corner near the potted palm . . ."

Brown looked. "Very attractive," he said.

"A moment, Monsieur." The other was gone.

Brown wondered vaguely if the girl was actually a fellow guest or part of the accommodations offered by the Satellite City Authority. Evidently, it was difficult to remain without companionship in the orbital hotel.

He came to his feet upon their approach. He wondered at the protocol. Shouldn't he have been taken to her table and introduced?

Warren said smoothly, "Mademoiselle Beauregard, may I present Monsieur Brown? Forgive me, the head chef quite insists that haut cuisine must not be enjoyed alone."

"Very kind of you," she murmured and looked into Brown's face, questioningly.

He held a chair for her, even as Warren took off, beaming.

For his taste, she had looked better at a distance. Not that she hadn't utilized everything with which nature had provided her. She had long, straight, semi-blonde hair which fell in a straight gloss. Her eyes were an improbable blue, so that he decided she must wear contact lenses. Her skin texture was such that it seemed a grainless plastic. Her clothes must have cost a mint. Nevertheless, her face held what amounted to an almost lifeless indifference, a negative response. His first reaction was to wonder why she had come to join him. He didn't get the impression that his masculine charm had overwhelmed her.

However, she said, in a slightly high voice which he couldn't decide emanated from nature or from nervousness—and she didn't seem the nervous type, by any stretch, "I suppose this is something like being on shipboard. Informality is the rule."

"Certainly. How pleasant of you to join me."

She said, "Your first day?"

"My first few hours."

"I've been here longer but this is the first time I've dined outside my room."

He said, in the way of make-conversation, "What brings you to Satellite City . . . Miss Beauregard?"

"Briget."

"Harold," he said.

There was an intent something in her expression that he hadn't caught earlier, back and beyond the indifference. She suddenly seemed to attempt to hide it and brought her eyes down to her fingers, on the table.

"When I graduated, Daddy gave me carte blanche in my choice of a vacation." She smiled a tight, meaningless smile. "I don't think he quite expected me to choose Satellite City. Not at these prices. However, a promise made is a debt unpaid, or however it goes. And here I am."

She seemed a bit older than would have fit in with a graduation, however, he shrugged inwardly. Possibly she had taken a doctor's or even an academecian's degree. You could spend a good many years in school in this age. You could spend your life.

"And you?" she said.

He made with a half smile. "I suppose I came up for the thrill. Every year that goes by on earth, the world becomes safer. In the old days one used to be able to go to hell in his own way, if you'll pardon the expression. Now there seem to be guard rails, or the equivalent, every place where you are in danger of stubbing your toe. I thought possibly that space would be different."

"And do you find it so?" she said. The slightly shrill quality in her voice irritated him, and he was irritated at himself at the fact. He wasn't going to marry this girl, nor possibly ever see her again after this evening. Why should he care if her voice was less than the slumbrous throatiness of some current Tri-Di sex symbol?

He indicated the room. "I've never seen a layout as

luxurious as this in the fondest fantasies of a Tri-Di producer. But so far as it being thrilling . . ."

She said, "You'll have to spend an hour or so in the free fall gym. And also get a guide to take you around the city in a shuttle run-about. They'll even let you pilot, if you wish. You go from one wheel to another, or to the hydroponic tank compartments. Or you can make arrangements to get a spacesuit and walk about on the outside—always with a guide, of course."

"You make me feel like a tourist," Brown said.

A girl carrying a gilded stool and wearing a trim, very short-skirted waitress outfit, approached them and said, pertly, "You are ready to order, Madam, Monsieur?" She even had a touch of French accent.

"Of course," Brown said.

She sat the stool next to the table, sat upon it, brought forth a tiny mike from her trim little apron and looked at them expectantly.

"A cocktail; perhaps a dry Sherry, perhaps a Brut Champagne?"

Brown looked at his companion. "Champagne?"

"No. Nothing." She made an artificial moue. "Champagne gives me acidosis."

Brown went back to the waitress. "Nor for me. May we have the menu?"

"I am sorry. There is no menu, Monsieur. The Galaxy Room can serve you anything you wish."

He looked at her. "Oh? Suppose I ordered a buffalo steak?"

"American buffalo, Monsieur, or water buffalo?"

He closed his eyes momentarily, opened them again to look at his dinner companion. "What would you like?"

A very faint gleam of amusement managed to break through her air of boredom. She said, "They must have absolutely endless storage compartments in connection with the kitchens. If I had the nerve, I'd order South African toasted locusts, but I'm afraid they'd have them. I've adopted a policy of leaving it to the chef. Which is exactly what I shall do now." She looked at the waitress and said, "I think I prefer Scandinavian cusine tonight."

"Yes, Madam." The girl murmured into her mike, then looked at Brown. "Monsieur, would you like me to make suggestions?"

"No," Brown said in resignation. "Surprise me. I'm fond of Italian food, especially Venetian. Soave wine. I assume you have it?"

"Of course, Monsieur. Will Bertani be acceptable?"

He looked at her. "You have Soave Bertani?"

"It is said that our cellars are as extensive as any . . . anywhere, Monsieur."

When she had gone, Brown looked at his companion and said, with a shake of his head, "No wonder people retire here."

She said, indifferently, once again, "You'll find out why they don't when you're charged for that wine."

"That's right. Drinks are one of the extras, aren't they?"

He was already weary of her. If he'd had good sense, he would have refused the *maitre d'* offer to provide him with a dining companion. He wasn't here to meet women.

The table center sank and returned with their initial dishes and his bottle of the slightly efferescent, faintly greenish in color light wine. It was superbly chilled, exactly right.

His initial dish was Prosciutto ham, that dark, spicy Italian product sliced tissue paper thin and served with figs and melon. It was unbelievably superlative. Her hor d'ouevres were principally half a dozen varieties of sil, and several Danish type smorrebrod open-faced sand-wiches. Disinterested, she barely touched the food.

She nibbled at her course after course and it came to him that she had a lean and hungry look, as Ceasar put it, but she had little interest in food.

He supposed that he could have suggested one of the bars or night spots following dinner, but he didn't feel up to more of her company. When they had finished their dessert, he went through the usual amenities, of-fered to escort her to her suite, was politely turned down, said his goodbyes and made his way over to the door where Warren presided.

VI

"Monsieur's dinner was acceptable?"

"Excellent," Brown said. "Where is the main casino, Warren?"

Warren beamed. "It adjoins the Galaxy Room, Monsieur." He indicated a double door at the far side of the dining room.

"It's open now, I assume?"

"The Casino opens at ten in the morning, Monsieur and remains open until two a.m."

Brown made his way to the gambling rooms, the doors sliding silently open before him upon his approach.

It was still only slightly after nine-thirty, but the extensive rooms were well packed with players, most of them in evening dress, a good many of the women, particularly the more elderly, laden with gems. Brown had never been an admirer of jewelry. For him, the more expensive it was, the more it looked like junk. He preferred a ten pseudo-dollar piece of costume jewelry, in good taste, to a diamond tiara.

For the time, he didn't bother to acquire chips with which to enter the play, but drifted about. He recognized every game he could remember ever having seen in gambling casinos; craps, blackjack, roulette, baccarat, faro, chuck-a-luck, slot machines, keno, a wheel of fortune; and even a few he hadn't run into before.

He stood before one of these. It was similar to a birdcage suspended on an axis and enclosed in a heavy bell-like glass. There were ten dice on the bottom of the cage, which was strategically located in the middle of the largest room, as though a place of prestige. There were none of the playing tables very near by.

A voice next to him said, "Feeling lucky, Mr. Brown?"

Brown turned. It was Antony Berch, the Protective officer who had relieved him of his gyro-jet pistol earlier.

"Why, I haven't begun to play as yet. I haven't any chips. I was wondering how this thing worked."

The younger man, who was in evening dress now, rather than uniform, was still polite to the point of unctuousness, and still cold of eye. He indicated a stall. "You can purchase chips over there at the auto-cashier. Simply put your identity card in the slot and order what you wish."

"I have no account in Satellite City."

Berch smiled. "An account in any bank in the world is valid here, Mr. Brown. The transfer will be made immediately."

Brown went over to the stall, brought out his pocket phone with his identity card sunk into its cover and put it in the indicated slot. He put his thumb on the identification square on the screen and then said, "A thousand dollars from my account in the Grundbank of Geneva, Switzerland."

The screen said, "Carried out, Mr. Brown." There was a clattering, somewhat similar to a slot machine paying off.

He reached down and scooped up the chips. There were ten of them. White. And each was marked, $100. He looked at them blankly for a moment, then up at the screen. "I'd prefer smaller denomination chips, than these."

"We are sorry, Mr. Brown. White chips are the smallest denomination utilized in the casino."

He hissed softly between his teeth at that, but turned and rejoined Antony Berch who awaited him at the unfamiliar gambling device.

"Okay," Brown said. "How does it work?"

The other smiled. "It's a sucker game, Mr. Brown. You might call it the one armed bandit to end all one-armed bandits. You don't have a chance of a chance at this one. But you'd be surprised how many try." He indicated. "You put a white chip in the slot there."

"And how much does it pay off, if I win?"

"A million to one."

Brown blinked at him. "The smallest chip you have in this casino is one hundred pseudo-dollars."

The other nodded. "The amount you win is one hundred million pseudo-dollars."

"Don't be ridiculous."

Berch smiled ruefully and pointed at the ten dice in the bottom of the birdcage. "You put your chip in and touch that button and the cage flips over, tossing the ten dice. If all ten come up sixes, then you win, a million to one."

"They could never pay off," Brown rapped.

"Ah, but they could, and would. This casino is backed by all the resources of the Satellite City Authority. But they're not going to have to pay off. Consider the odds for a moment, Mr. Brown. If you throw one die, you have one chance in six that it will come up six. If you throw two dice the percentage is one in thirty-six that both will come up sixes. Have three dice and, let me see, the percentage becomes two hundred and sixteen to one that all there will come up sixes."

"And using ten dice?"

The other smiled. "That's why the casino will never have to pay off. The percentage of chance that all ten will come up sixes is more than six hundred million to one. It is the worst percentage of any gambling device in the world."

"What happens if only nine come up sixes?"

"Nothing. You lose. You have to get all ten."

Fascinated, Harold Brown put one of his chips in the slot and touched the button. The bird cage flipped completely over. Two of the dice showed sixes.

Berch said, "It never fails, sir. I don't know of a single guest who has ever come into the orbital hotel who doesn't give it a try." He chuckled, sourly. "I've given it a try—just once. And I'm not in the bracket of our guests here."

Brown gave a short laugh. "Well, you can add me to the sucker list. But only this once."

A trimly uniformed girl came up and said something softly to Antony Berch who nodded and excused himself to Brown and followed her.

Brown looked at the birdcage and its dice for a moment, and shook his head. One of the other gamblers came up and put a chip in and pressed the button. His face didn't change when only one six turned up. Brown got the impression that this one had returned to the birdcage more than once.

Jiggling his nine remaining chips, he strode on, looking for some game a bit more austere and one with which he was at least moderately familiar.

He was intrigued by the extent to which the gambling rooms were automated. Even blackjack. The craps tables were some of the few that sported croupiers, but he had never particularly liked craps. Although he had never been much of a gambler, roulette had intrigued him on the few occasions he had visited the casinos on earth.

He had never seen an automated roulette wheel before but it was obviously no great departure. The one he stopped at had only two players, an elderly, evening dress clad, overly fat man, who sweated as he played, and consistently lost, and a young woman Brown at first took to be an Indian, due to her sari dress and rather dark complexion. She played earnestly and deftly and had a sizeable pile of blue chips before her. He couldn't figure out just what system she was using but evidently she was winning. He watched for a few moments, figuring out how the table operated. The ball was tossed automatically into the spinning wheel. At a given time, the table's screen announced, "*All bets terminated.*" When the ball settled into one of the 36 numbers, half and half red and black, and, of course, odd and even, or into the one white number, which gave the house its percentage, all squares upon which bets had been placed sank into the depths of the layout and those that had won rose again with the correct amount of win.

It was all very efficient.

Brown finally stepped up and put one of his white chips on *odd*, a one-to-one bet, if you ignored the possibility of the roulette ball dropping into the white zero slot.

The other two ignored him and placed their own bets.

He won, they lost. He let his bet ride and the next spin won again so that he now has four chips on odd. He let it ride again, won again and had eight chips on odd. The red faced elderly type had been cleaned out and swore a filthy oath, supposedly under his breath, but clear enough to be heard, and made off.

The girl looked at Brown and said, "You seem to be having a streak. I ought to ride along with you."

He realized that in spite of her sari, she was either Eruopean or American. Few Caucasians ever learn to wear the sari, that most graceful of all women's wear. Invariably, they look gawky compared to their Hindu sisters. This one wore it as though born to the flowing dress.

He said, "Don't do it. My streaks never last."

"Wrong attitude," she said, and began placing her bet again. Evidently, the conversation was over.

He picked up his winnings, decided to switch and wagered one chip on red. He lost and put down two chips for the next spin. He lost again and put down four.

She looked at him and shook her head. "You're playing the Martingale system. It's the stupidest in the book."

"I beg your pardon."

She said patiently, "Look. You're doubling up. You bet one and lose, so you bet two and if you lose, you bet four, and if you lose, you bet eight. You figure that sooner or later you're going to win. But suppose you lose, say, six times in a row, which isn't at all hard? You've then got 64 chips on the line. Then if you win, you know how much profit you've got? Exactly one chip. It's a sucker's system."

He looked at her. "Everybody's been telling me I'm a sucker tonight. A few minutes ago I tried to win a hundred million pseudo-dollars."

She snorted contempt. "The birdcage. It's the biggest con in Satellite City. Six hundred million to one against you winning. If you're going to gamble, pick a game that gives you reasonable percentages."

She was very brunette and with the cream-olive skin of the Greek, Southern Italian and Andulusian Spanish. She was an extremely attractive woman, somewhere, he decided in her early thirties. She had the most beautiful teeth he could ever remember having seen and her mouth's red was of nature, rather than cosmetics. He was prone to brunettes. She also had the air of the wealthy who have been wealthy many generations, so many that wealth was no longer thought about.

He said, "Such as what?"

She placed another bet. "In actuality, craps, if you know your percentages, are probably as good a bet as any. You can get it down to as little as seven tenths of one percent against you. An expert can get blackjack down to six tenths. Slot machines are stupid. Here in this casino they give you the best odds I've ever heard about, but they're still ten percent against you. Play over a period of time and for every thousand you put in, you take out nine hundred. Baccarat isn't too bad, about 1.26 percent against you."

Brown said, interested, "You seem to have looked into it. How about roulette?"

She won her bet and picked up her winnings and looked at him, twisting her mouth in a grimace. "The spinning wheel is my weakness. In the Nueva Las Vegas and other American casinos they have a zero and a double-zero, which gives 5.26 percentage against you. Here in Satellite City, as with the Common Europe casinos, you have only the one zero, so the percentage is two percent against."

"Okay. My doubling up system is stupid. What system are you using?"

She flashed a quick gleaming smile. "It's called *Tiers de Tout,* a third of everything. It's based on the fact that if you play any gambling game long enough the house percentage finally beats you. So in the *Tiers de Tout* you don't play very long. You allow yourself a certain amount and either win fast, or go broke."

He liked her. "Okay, Great. Tell me about it."

She said, "You take your whole stake—say you start with nine chips—and divide it into two piles of three chips and six chips. You bet the three. If you lose, you bet the six. If you lose again, you're broke and call it a night."

"And if you win the first time?"

"You redivide the twelve chips into four and eight and bet the four. If you lose, you bet the eight. If you lose that one, you're broke."

"And if you win the eight bet?"

"Then you divide the sixteen chips and come up with five chips and eleven and start all over again."

Brown said, sceptically, "It seems to me that it wouldn't be hard to go broke awfully quickly. All you have to do is lose twice in a row."

"That's right. But if you win, you win fast and you make your pile before the house averages can get to you."

"You're on," he said, moving next to her. "Let's see how it goes. How much are those blue chips worth?"

"A thousand," she said.

"A thousand pseudo-dollars?"

"That's right." She must have had at least two hundred of them, in piles before her.

He hissed quietly between his teeth and duplicated her blue chips bet with three of his white ones. They won. He continued to follow her lead and they won again, and again.

From time to time, they'd take a loss and double up the bet. And invariably won.

His bets became large enough that the table began to

return him red chips, which were marked five hundred dollars, rather than the one hundred of the whites.

They were playing shoulder to shoulder.

Finally, she said, "All right. That's it for the night."

"How do you mean? We're hitting like insane."

"That's why we quit. Stick at it long enough and your lucky streak runs out and the house percentage takes over."

"Oh," he said, looking down at his respectable pile of red and white chips. "It seems a shame to quit now. We're getting rich."

She twisted her mouth slightly in deprecation. "We're already rich, or we wouldn't be here in Satellite City."

He looked at her. "Name's Brown. Harold."

"Gina. Gina Angel."

"Angel?" he said. "No cracks intended. You look like one in that gold sari. But I don't think I've ever heard the name before." He didn't know why he said it, but he did. "Are you an actress?"

She looked at him questioningly. "No. I'm not an actress."

"Well . . . what do you do?" He knew it was an asinine question, even as he asked it. Evidently, according to Scoop Ericsson, just about everybody in Satellite City protected their anonymity. You just didn't ask about such matters.

She said, "I own Satellite City."

VII

Had Miss Angel—he assumed she was a Miss, rather than a Mrs.—suddenly sprouted halo and wings and taken off in flight, she would have been hard put to set him back any further.

He decided it was a joke that hadn't quite come off and looked at her sizeable pile of blue chips and attempted to keep it going. "Well, you certainly own a considerable chunk of it, after tonight's luck."

"You haven't done so badly yourself," she said.

An impeccably clad young man drifted up, nonchalantly. He took Brown in with a sweep of his eyes and said to the girl, "Everything all right, Miss Angel?"

"Certainly, Vincent," she told him. She indicated her piles of chips. "Would you mind taking care of these for me?"

"Not at all, Miss Angel."

Brown's own accumulation wasn't such that he needed help. He took up his chips and said to her, "If it wasn't for your advice, I'd probably be busted by now. I owe you a drink."

Vincent looked at him expressionlessly.

But the girl flashed her ever-so-white teeth and said, "You're on. Between here and the bar I'll try to think up the most expensive drink in Satellite City."

She fell into step beside him. He had already made out the casino's sumptuous bar at the far end of the room.

On the way, they passed the automatic chip cashier where he had secured his ten white chips earlier.

She said, "Wouldn't you like to cash those in?"

He had put some of his chips in his pockets but he had both hands full as well. He said, "I thought I'd possibly play a little more, later."

"Oh no you don't." She snorted contempt. "I told you. If you play long enough the house percentage gets to you, sooner or later." She touched one finger to her lips. "Start again tomorrow night with the same amount you began with tonight and I'll teach you the *Noir* system. It's not quite so frenetic as the *Tiers de Tout*." She stopped before the auto-cashier.

"How does this work?" he said.

"Put your identity card in the slot there, and then dump your chips into the counter there. Your account will be credited."

He followed instructions and said mildly, "How do I know I'll get a square count?"

She laughed softly. "Satellite City does not make its profits by cheating the clientel, Mr. Brown. In fact, if there was any way of arranging for you to win—this *is* your first visit, isn't it?"

"Yes."

"If there was any way of arranging for you to win, that would be the thing to do. To insure your return and to encourage you to recommend Satellite City to your friends. You see, there are only a few thousand persons remaining in the world who can afford to visit here. The Authority needs good publicity."

"I was going to do that anyway. I had decided to tell them that in Satellite City angels went around in gold saris telling you how to make a mint in the casino."

"Thank you, kind sir, but just think what you would

have told them if you had lost. A floozy gave you poor advice and you lost your shirt."

They were to the bar and he found that three live bartenders presided, which was mildly surprising in itself. Satellite City seemed to be a combination of the ultra in automation and an anachronistic use of live personnel.

They stopped before the classic bartender. His smile bore just the correct amount of bonhomie but at the same time there was the withdrawn expression of the dispenser of cheer who seemingly isn't quite there, who most certainly hears nothing his customers are saying— unless they are talking directly to him, or particularly if they wish a good listener to whom to tell troubles.

This one said, "Good evening, Miss Angel. Good evening, sir."

Gina Angel said, "Good evening, Nicolo. The usual, please."

Brown said, "Pseudo-whiskey and water."

While the bartender was making the drinks, Harold Brown said to the girl, "And is *the usual* the most expensive drink in Satellite City?"

She had to laugh. "I don't know." She cocked her head a bit. "Pseudo-whiskey for someone who can afford the admittedly astronomical prices here?"

He shrugged. "It has been brought home to me, by the resident publicity man, among others, that the scientific boys in the laboratories have discovered how to manufacture much better grog than ever came out of the distilleries of Scotland. Drinking real Scotch is a status symbol. I am far enough along in my field that I don't need status symbols."

The drinks had come, hers evidently based on champagne, and they toasted each other. "More luck," she said. "And what is your field, Mr. Brown? You asked me if I was an actress. Are you an actor?" She took a tiny sip from her glass.

He smiled ruefully. "I suppose that I'm the last of the entrepreneurs—or one of the last."

"What does that mean?"

"Well, what with the Soviet Complex taking up nearly half of the world, and the Welfare States of the West taking up most of the rest, the room for the old style financial robber baron has shrunken drastically. However, there are still a few places in the world where a good thing presents itself from time to time. I've heard that Satellite City is one of them, which is a reason I came to take a look."

"I see. And what are the other reasons?"

He took down some his drink. "The thrill. It's old hat to you, possibly, but for someone who has never been in space it's something new in a world that doesn't have many thrills left."

"We seem to be kindred spirits. What sort of thrills do you go in for, Mr. Brown?"

He shifted his shoulders in deprecation. "Just about all of the sports. Of recent years I've gone in especially for hunting, preferably dangerous game."

"If I'm not mistaken, that's rather difficult to find these days, isn't it? And with gyro-jet rifles, and even lasers, it can't be as dangerous as all that."

"Have you ever stalked a Bengal tiger with a twenty-two pistol, Miss Angel?"

"Good heavens, no. Isn't a twenty-two one of those very smallest calibers?"

"The smallest," he said, taking another swallow of his pseudo-whiskey.

Her eyes were round. "When did this take place? And where?"

He shrugged it off. "Two or three years ago, in Bengal —India, of course."

She nodded as she finished her drink. She put her glass down definitely. "So you are an actor, after all."

"How do you mean?"

"If you stalked a Bengal tiger within the last two or three years, Mr. Brown, it must have been in a zoo. The last Bengal tiger to be shot in the wild was some five years ago. A rather motheaten specimen taken on the estate of the former Maharajah of Berhampore. At the time, the conservation people went into a tissy. Evidently, it was the last tiger in the region."

He looked at her speechlessly.

She said, "I was the one who shot it. But not with a twenty-two pistol, Mr. Brown. Thanks for the drink. Good evening."

She turned to go but then looked over her shoulder. "Oh, that offer to teach you the *Noir* roulette system tomorrow night. I just remembered a prior engagement."

He had cursed himself inwardly, after she left. It had been stupidly done. It was one thing, giving such a story to some pickup in a bar in, say, Greater Washington, but to the type of sophisticate you met in Satellite City you were taking a chance. He had taken it and lost.

Well, possibly it was all for the best. He hadn't come up here to meet attractive women, or in any other manner be brought to the attention of the other guests in the orbital hotel of Satellite City.

His first inclination had been to call it a night and to go to bed but on second thought decided to check out the public rooms of the hotel a bit more. He had tucked the pamphlet which was the Satellite City directory into his inner jacket pocket. Now he brought it forth and turned to the charts of the orbital hotel. The directions were easily followed and he made his way to the entertainment offerings.

There were three restaurants, besides the Galaxy Room, all on much more of an intimate nature than the larger dining hall. One was Oriental, one European with a French motif, and one American. He did little more than peer inside. Only a few tables were occupied at this hour. Evidently, Earth-side time was largely followed and based on the hour that applied in London.

He stopped off, too, in several of the bars and even had an ale in the one designed to resemble a British pub. The effect was carried out even to the extent of having a barmaid with a Cockney accent, and English style pork pies in the way of snacks. He was too replete with the large Italian dinner to give them a try. The pub exuded the friendly atmosphere for which such establishments were famous, but he didn't encourage communication with the others lining the bar.

He had thought to sit in for awhile at one of the nightspots and see what Satellite City offered in the way of shows, but of a sudden he was bored and tired and made his way back to his suite. He noted that traffic in the corridors was already thinning out. Evidently, very late hours were not the rule here.

The identity screen of Suite K-1 picked him up and the door opened automatically at his approach. He began to shrug out of his jacket, even as he entered, but then pulled up abruptly.

The companion of Al Rich, of the Satellite City staff, was seated there in one of the room's two comfort chairs. What had Rich called him? Rocky.

Rocky looked up, no higher than Brown's chest, but for the moment said nothing.

Brown scowled and said, "What in the hell are you doing here? This place seems to have all the privacy of the New Orange Bowl."

Rocky said softly, "Mind closing the door?"

Brown looked at him. "Why?"

"Why not?"

Brown took him in for another long moment. Finally, "That sounds like a good question." He closed the door. "Okay. To what do I owe the honor?"

Rocky's eyes went around the suite, unseeingly, "I thought I might do you a favor." He shifted stocky shoulders in his evening jacket. He didn't really belong in an evening jacket.

"In return for what? And what kind of a favor?"

Rocky shrugged again. His eyes shifted again. "In return for a favor, Mr. . . . Brown. Say a financial favor."

Harold Brown went over to the small autobar and dialed himself a pseudo-whiskey and water, even as he did so, realizing that he didn't truly want it. He wanted a clear head.

He said, "Listen. So far as I know, there's precious little in the way of a favor I need. Everything is going fine."

"I might know some things you don't know."

"It's your top. Start spinning it."

Rocky's eyes went down to his feet, checking his shoe shine, evidently. He said, finally, "Mr. . . . Brown, it's all very nice up here—if you have the money. You have the money. I haven't. I'm a working joe."

"Okay. Great."

"But you realize some of the things you can buy up here. They're kind of hard to get other places."

"That's obvious. What's this mysterious favor?"

"You don't sound so favorable, Mr. . . . Brown."

"I am not. Go on. Let's have your pitch. I've heard pitches before, Rocky."

Rocky's eyes came up as far as Brown's chin, but no further. He said, "With a deal like this Satellite City, you gotta have some kinda tough boys to handle the rougher edges, like."

"And . . ."

Rocky sighed and came to his feet. "I can see where we're not getting anywhere. I'll see you around, Mr. . . . . Brown."

"Do that."

Brown turned and watched him to the door, but didn't see him out. The other moved as gracefully as before, in spite of his heftiness. Harold Brown wondered if he had ever been a pugilist—or perhaps a chorus boy. He also wondered if he hadn't made a mistake in not hearing the other out, and giving him his bribe. Well, it was too late for that now. For some reason, Rocky irritated him.

The following day he conducted himself as he assumed every other first-tripper to Satellite City would.

After a superlative breakfast in his suite, delivered automatically to the table, he brought forth the directory pamphlet and looked up the sightseeing opportunities. Had he wished, he could have had an individual guide and been escorted about in an individual shuttle craft, however, he decided upon one of the group tours, feeling that most likely he would be more anonymous going around with a half dozen or more others than being alone. One tour began in the reception hall of the orbital hotel at ten hours and he made his way there, retracing the route along which the hip-swishing Gertrude had brought him the day before.

He approached the desk, and the smiling young thing

who so obviously was prepared to grant his slightest wish. He was getting to the point of thinking that the Satellite City service was just a little *too* perfect, all the personnel just a little too bright and brisk and ultra-helpful.

He said, "I'd like to take the ten o'clock tour. I'm Harold Brown in Suite K-1."

"Of course, Mr. Brown," she beamed at him. "It will be leaving in a matter of moments. Over there. Your guide's name is Charles Ruby."

Brown started in the indicated direction and then almost came to a halt. The maroon uniformed guide was already cheerfully addressing a gathering of six or seven. What made Brown hesitate was the presence in the group of Briget Beauregard, of the shrill voice and the air of lifeless indifference, his dinner companion in the Galaxy Room the night before.

His feeling of irritation in her company came over him again. Well, the hell with it. He was under no compulsion to continue the brief relationship.

He came up to the group and nodded to her and said, "Miss Beauregard."

She nodded back, politely enough, but then her eyes returned to the guide who evidently was in the midst of a brief description of just what they were to do between ten and lunch time. This tour didn't include the orbital hotel, evidently, but only those areas of Satellite City involved in the science wheel, the orbital hospital and the larger of the hydroponic tanks, the farms of the space town.

When they were ushered to the shuttle craft which was to take them from one wheel to the other, Brown avoided getting too near Briget Beauregard, not wanting to be seated next to her. Two male attendants fell in be-

74

hind them and followed into the airlock up against which was snuggled their little space bus. The airlock hatch closed behind them and they shuffled into the shuttlecraft where Guide Ruby directed them to free fall chairs into which they were bound by the two efficient attendants.

Brown was seated next to a plump matron who chattered her way all the distance to the science wheel, and through the docking there. She had made the trip before, evidently, several times, and was not adverse to telling all about it, usually contradicting the guide's efforts to accomplish the same.

Devil take it, he told himself, under his breath, another Frank Cunningham. He seemed to be running into a whole series of self-appointed guides; including, now that he thought about it, Gina Angel, the expert on gambling percentages. Well, at least, she seemingly had known what she was expounding. Now that he thought about it, he felt like kicking himself all over again as a reward for making such a fool of himself. In spite of his desire for anonymity, the girl was such that he would have liked to have seen more of her.

The tour had its fascinations, but not to the extent he had expected. The trip from Earth-side, the landing at the space dock, and the shuttling over to the orbital hotel of the day before had taken most of the keen first edge off the excitement of space flight.

The guide was good and Harold Brown caught a subtle something that was obviously part of his duty when Ruby mentioned, seemingly in innocent passing, that both the working personnel of the orbiting hospital and that of the science wheel were most cooperative in greeting visiting vacationists from the hotel.

Ruby said, "The day of the tax free foundation is just

about over, Earth-side. In fact, just about anything tax free is over, Earth-side, which I am sure bothers you folks more than it does me.

He got a few sour laughs out of that.

"However, the same thing doesn't apply here, you know. The Satellite City Authority is highly in favor of those spirited philantropists who wish to help along the cause of medicine or the other sciences. Just last week a long time resident of the orbiting hospital donated a full third of his sizeable fortune to research into some of the more obscure cancer viruses."

He continued, still as though in passing, "And last year, a gentleman whose name I am not free to reveal but who had managed to transfer a considerable amount of his fortune from Brazil, before the sweeping national-ization there, formed a tax free trust through the Satellite City Bank which will keep his large family in affluence so long as money is still utilized anywhere on Earth."

From the side of his eyes, Brown noticed that several of his fellow tourists looked thoughtful.

He decided, dourly, that he wished he owned a chunk of the stock of the Satellite City Authority. Which brought to mind that he had never heard just how it was owned. Was it possible to buy in? Off hand, he couldn't think of a better investment. The thing was obviously booming. Shuttling through it like this brought home just how much construction was going on.

It seemed to be his day for running into people he had already met. While following the guide down one of the corridors of the ultra-sterile orbiting hospital, he was amused to see Frank Cunningham, white-clad, with an armful of towels over his arm, emerge from a patient's room.

A male nurse—or less.

Brown said to him, "Hello, Frank."

Frank Cunningham flushed. "Oh, good morning, Mr. Brown." He bobbed his head, for all the world like a British lackey of yesteryear, and hurried on his way. Gone was the equality of being passengers together on the spaceship from Earth.

He also ran into the public relations man, Scoop Ericsson, while they were being conducted about the science wheel. Guide Ruby was having his work cut out to even begin describing what it was that the various laboratories were working upon. In fact, Brown inwardly came to the conclusion that Ruby himself had only the vaguest of ideas.

Brown gave up trying to understand the ramifications of biologists working in vacuum conditions and said to Ericsson, from the side of his mouth, "Suppressed any good news today, Scoop?"

The other grinned at him. "Ha! This is the one section of Satellite City where they don't want it suppressed. The publicity hound is not unknown among even the top mucky-mucks in the world of science, Mr, . . . Mr. . . ." He grinned again. "See, I've forgotten your name."

Brown said, "Continue the good work, friend."

They were taken inward into any of the wheels only so far as where one quarter earth gravity applied. Evidently, some of the space tourists were either afraid of, or in danger in, complete free fall. Charles Ruby let them know that there were other tours for those who wished the experience but, especially for the first time, it was recommended that each sightseer have an individual guide. One fourth gravity seemed bad enough. You could keep your feet, after a preliminary period in half gravity and a quick course of instruction by Ruby, but the more elderly, in particular, weren't exactly happy.

Brown made a point of not getting too close to Briget Beauregard but he noticed that she seemed bored more than he'd think called for. After all, why had she come to Satellite City if not for exactly this? Though, from what she had said, she had already made similar tours.

His running into others he had already met continued upon their return to reception, in the hotel. The bright and brisk airline hostess type who had seen him to his suite upon his arrival was there.

She flashed him her come-on smile and said, "You're sure there's nothing I can do for you, Mr. Brown? Just anything at all? We're here to serve."

He shook his head. "Thank you . . ." her name was stitched over her fulsome left breast ". . . Gertrude." He passed on in the direction of his quarters, noticing that she was looking after him, frowning slightly, and it occurred that she was wondering whether or not she was losing her grip.

Well, he told himself, once more, what she had to offer wasn't the thing for which he had come to Satellite City.

He had lunch in the Oriental restaurant and was impressed again by the ultra-luxurious qualities of Satellite City. He then went back to the suite and collapsed into sleep. He had taken a crack at the free fall gym in mind for later in the day, but there seemed to be something in the Satellite City atmosphere that was conducive to slumber and he put in more time at napping than he had figured upon.

When he awoke, his feeling of repletion from the meal was gone, but so was ambition to do much sightseeing. He had half a mind to go on back to the casino and have another try at gambling. After all, he hadn't done so badly the night before, although, come to think of it, that *Tier de Tout* system of Gina Angel's was a little rich for his blood. You had to be the type where going bust made no difference to take those chances, and he wasn't exactly in that category.

He was saved the decision when his identity screen buzzed.

The fact was that of Al Rich, the suave type with the empty eyes. So many seemed to have empty eyes here in Satellite City.

Brown opened up and looked at the other quizzically.

Al Rich said, "The time has come, Mr. Brown."

The husky Rocky stood behind him.

Harold Brown stood to one side and let them enter and closed the door. He took a deep breath and said, "What time?"

Al Rich went over to a chair and sat down and looked at him speculatively. Rocky remained near the door, standing, his eyes away into nothingness.

Rich said, "Still want to go through with the contract?"

"Is that what you call it, a contract?" Brown looked over at Rocky suggestively.

Rich said, "Of necessity, a certain minimum number of persons have to know about it all, Mr. Brown. Rocky is one. The question is, do you still want to go through with the contract, in short, the privilege of . . . ah, shooting a pretty young girl, expensively dressed. Ah, were there any other requirements?"

"No. Those were the requirements," Brown said, his voice tight. He took another long breath. "Yes. I still want to go through with it."

The expression on the other's face was still speculative.

Rocky had no expression whatsoever, as though he had gone through similar scenes and conversations a score of times over.

Brown said, "What would happen if I decided not to go through with it?"

Al Rich shook his head. "Nothing. You'd simply stay on here for as long as you wished, and then return Earthside."

"How about the hundred thousand pseudo-dollars?"

"I believe that was explained to you. A contract is a contract. We've lived up to our part of it."

Brown said, "What am I supposed to do, strangle her? Your Protective officers took my gun."

Rich said, without looking at his assistant, "Rocky."

Rocky put a hand inside his jacket and brought forth a pistol and tendered it to Harold Brown, butt first.

Brown looked down at it. "It's a laser."

"That's right," Rich said, "and with just enough of a charge in it for one full shot. It's also permanently jimmied to minimum range. We don't want you burning a hole into space."

"Suppose I miss that first shot?"

"With a laser? Besides, you told us you were an experienced hunter."

"Okay. Where do I find her?"

"She's in the suite next to this one. Suite L-1. I suggest you take not too very long."

Al Rich gave Brown one more speculative look with his cold eyes, then came to his feet and motioned with his head to Rocky. They left without further words.

Harold Brown threw the gun's power pack clip and inspected it. There was a red dot at the top, indicating it held charge. He inspected the gun expertly. So far as he could see, it was in perfect shape. He flicked the charge back into the gun's butt and rammed it home with the heel of his right hand.

For the moment, he tucked the gun into his belt and went into the bedroom. He retrieved his shoulder holster rig from the dresser drawer into which he had tossed it the day before, removed his jacket and shrugged into the harness. He tried the laser pistol in it and found it fit reasonably well, although the holster had been designed for a slightly smaller gyro-jet gun.

He got back into his jacket and stood before the mirror and tried a couple of quick draws. They seemed to come off to satisfaction. Okay. Great. Now to go and see if the girl was really there.

He left his suite and looked up and down the corridor. No one was in sight. He walked quickly to the door of the suite next to his. Suite L-1.

The identity screen was evidently tuned to him. The door opened as he approached and he went in.

The living room was almost identical to his own.

On the couch sat Briget Beauregard.

They both said, "You?" as though they had rehearsed it.

For once, Miss Beauregard did not look indifferent. Her face was intent, her very blue eyes wide. She wore an expensive, silver-shimmering evening gown and the bag on her lap matched it.

Harold Brown closed the door behind him and turned and faced her again.

He remembered Rocky's warning about the fact that he was dealing with tough elements here in Satellite City, but he said, "Do you know why you're here?"

Her voice was an octave or so even higher than usual.

"Yes," she said, "although I didn't expect it to be you. I paid fifty-thousand pseudo-dollars for the privilege of shooting a young man. I'm glad it's a pig like you."

Her hand darted into her bag. She fumbled for a moment, then came out with a laser pistol the twin of his own. She held it in both hands, directed it at him, and pulled the trigger.

A tiny beam of light lanced from it and struck him full in the chest.

PART TWO

VIII

He felt nothing whatsoever.

She scowled down at the gun then directed it at him again, once again holding it with both hands. She pulled trigger once more but this time without any result. She pulled harder. There was a trickle of spital at the side of her mouth.

"Die!" she screamed at him.

He licked lips that had gone very dry and finally shook his head at her. "You evidently got cut rates," he told her. "I ponied up one hundred thousand to do the same to you."

The door to the bedroom opened and Al Rich entered, closely followed by the inevitable Rocky.

Rich looked at Harold Brown. "Why didn't you make your try, Mr. Bader? That draw of hers was one of the slowest on record. Surely you could have beaten that."

The girl began to run at them, her hand held forward like claws, her carmine red fingernails seemingly blood-covered.

Rich snapped, "Rocky!"

The husky moved with deceptive speed, had no difficulty pinning her arms behind her as she spat and mouthed obscenities.

Al Rich looked back at the man who called himself Harold Brown. "Well?"

"The name's Brown."

"No, it's not. The name's Bader, Rex Bader, and there

are some very strange things about you. Why didn't you make your try, Mr. Bader?"

"I never intended to. Of course, I didn't think the girl was going to be dealt the same hand. You surprised me there. However, all I wanted to see was *if* it could be done."

"Just pure curiosity?"

"I suppose you could call it that."

"You have an expensive curiosity, Mr. Bader." Al Rich turned and called into the bedroom, "Joe."

Two of the maroon-uniformed Satellite City employees entered. They took the girl off Rocky's hands. One of them deftly pressed a hypodermic into her arm. She was still obviously over the edge.

Al Rich, sauve and polite as ever, said to her, "Miss Beauregard, these two men are going to take you to the orbiting hospital. You need help. You'll receive it. Some of the world's most advance psychiatrists are with us. Treatment is fast and good. In a few days, you will be a much happier woman and have no memory of this whatsoever."

She began to shrill again, but suddenly went blank, as the hypo evidently hit her. The two attendants led her from the room.

Al Rich turned back again and said, "Sit down, Mr. Bader. Would you like a drink?"

"I could use one."

"Rocky."

Rocky went over to the autobar. He looked at Rex Bader, no higher than the chest. "Whiskey?"

"Fine." Rex Bader slumped down into a comfort chair. He said, "Wow."

Rocky brought him his drink, a double, neat. He handed a second glass, this one a long drink with ice, to his superior. Rocky had ordered nothing for himself. He backed away and leaned against a wall.

Rex Bader knocked back half of the whiskey. Then he looked at Al Rich who had seated himself on the couch that the girl had occupied earlier.

He said, "If I had made my try, as you called it, would you have bundled me off to the nut factory too?"

"Of course. Anybody far enough gone to want to knock somebody off for the thrill needs medical care, Mr. Bader."

"You sound as though you've been through this before."

The other nodded, "We have. You see, the Satellite City Authority cultivates the reputation of being free-wheeling, of being able to supply just about any far-out desire a well-heeled thrill seeker might want. It pays off. Within reason, you can go to pot in your own way here. But, in actuality, you have to keep it within reason."

"And this same thing happens every time?"

"Not exactly. You see, it's one thing some crackpot, Earth-side, deciding he wants the thrill of bumping someone off. But the closer he gets to the actual event, the colder his feet usually get. We make every effort to allow the guest to back out. Most of them do. We throw them in contact with their supposed victim, as you were thrown in contact with Miss Beauregard. Sometimes they're even attracted to each other. Then, when the opportunity is supposedly presented for the kill, they seldom press the trigger. They seldom even find out the guns are jimmied.

"But before that ever happens, we come around several times and ask whether they're sure they want to go through with the contract. Rocky comes around and tries to throw a slight scare into the guest by hinting that something off-beat is going on. Oh, we do all we can to chill the thing before it ever gets as far as Miss Beauregard took it."

"Why allow them to make such a contract at all?"

Al Rich smiled wanly. "Two reasons, Mr. Bader. We charge a fifty to a hundred thousand pseudo-dollars which is a nice little amount even in Satellite City. But, more important, in the long run, we bring highly wealthy newcomers to Satellite City for the first time. They see our facilities, and almost all like them. They come back, for the gambling, the girls, the boys, and the other attractions. They learn about the banking facilities and the Bourse, and many open accounts. They are only a few thousand potential guests of our resort in the whole world, Mr. Bader, and one of our big difficulties is to get them up here for the first time. Most of them then become repeats. I strongly suspect that Briget Beauregard will become a repeat, once her psychosomatic twist has been cured." He shrugged slightly. "Possibly you will too, Mr. Bader . . . possibly."

"At a hundred thousand a throw?"

"That was for your special contract. From now on, it's only five thousand a round trip. But we're not sure about you, Mr. Bader."

"How did you learn my name?"

"We had *that* the day you walked into the Satellite City Authority Building in Tangier. We got your thumbprint and photographs there in Francisco Byass' office. But that's when you became unique. You have no dossier in the International Computer Data Banks, Mr. Bader, and the one in the American National Data Banks is so restricted as to be meaningless. Practically nothing beyond your name and age is available without a Priority One and although we have considerable in the way of resources, it takes time to crack a Priority One dossier. Time and money. But that's not what really set us back, Mr. Bader."

"Oh?"

Al Rich shook his head. "I have never even heard of an unlimited bank account before. Not even in Switzerland. Not even here in Satellite City. Your account in the Grundbank in Geneva is unlimited. Mr. Bader. How can it possibly be?"

"I'm afraid that's my business. So far as my dossier is concerned, if you have enough pull and enough pseudo-dollars to scatter around, you can make arrangements to give your dossier a high priority. I thought it worth the effort, and the money."

Al Rich said, "If you've finished your drink, do you mind coming along, Mr. Bader?"

"Where to?"

"To see the Don."

"And who the hell is the Don?"

"The senior official of the Satellite City Authority. He wished to see you, no matter what the outcome of this little drama."

"Suppose I don't want to see him? I've about decided to go on back to Earth on the next passenger rocket."

"Please. Let's keep this on an, ah, gentlemanly level. We have no intention of antagonizing our guests, Mr. Bader. Other things being equal, we hope you'll return and that you will also recommend our offerings to your friends. But if the Don wishes to see you, I'm afraid you'll have to see him." He hesitated before adding. "You've got a husky build but I suspect that Rocky, here, would be enough to coerce you into coming. If not, I can summon a couple of the Protective officers."

Rex Bader gave it up. "Okay. Let's go."

87

Outside the suite they went no further than a few yards to the nearest elevator. It was absolutely impossible for Rex Bader to adjust his mind to the fact that he was *sideways* so far as his relationship to Earth was concerned. Or, now that he thought about it, was he? He had no idea of what the angle of the Satellite City Orbial Hotel might be. Up was toward the axis; down was toward the rim; where his suite was located. Nothing else made any difference; where the Earth was, where the moon and stars were, or anything else.

They entered the elevator and went up. And it was further up than Rex Bader had gone thus far in the orbiting hotel. He could feel gravity falling away as they rose —or would *went in* be the better term?

It obviously meant nothing to his two companions. He wondered how much of their lives they spent in Satellite City. Did the permanent employees take long vacations Earth-side, or did they feel it necessary? That young fellow, Cunningham, he'd come up with on the rocket, had mentioned a lengthy vacation on Earth.

The elevator came to a halt and Al Rich said into the screen, "Al, Rocky and Mr. Bader."

The door opened and they stepped out into a corridor the twin of that on Rex Bader's level save that its curve was obviously tighter. They must, Bader decided, be fairly well in toward the axis of the wheel. However, he would have known that by the gravity. Had it not been for the experience of the guided tour that morning, he would have found it difficult to get used to it. It was certainly no more than one quarter normal.

A tall, thin man with a long disagreeable face and small, hard gray eyes stood next to a door that had no discernible identity screen.

When they approached he said, "Evening, Mr. Rich." He looked at Rocky, nodded, then looked at Rex Bader.

"We're expected, Dominick," Rich said.

"Yes, sir, I know." He went behind Rex Bader and slid his hands down his sides, after lightly patting the jacket and hip pockets. He touched the shoulder rig and his eyes went very icy. He ran a hand inside the jacket and brought forth the laser pistol.

He looked at Al Rich. "You know better than that, Mr. Rich."

Al Rich said easily, "Take a look at it, Dominick. It's a phoney. Jimmied. We use them below sometimes in special operations."

"I'll check it later," the thin one said. He tucked the pistol into a hip pocket and quickly frisked both Rocky and Al Rich in much the same manner he had Rex Bader. Evidently, they were clean. He said, "All right, Mr. Rich."

The door opened and Al Rich led the way into a room considerably larger than any Rex Bader had thus far seen in Satellite City, save for the public rooms. It was a living room, office combination so warm and humid that it was almost like taking a sauna bath. There were couches, several comfort chairs, an old-fashioned manual bar set in one carner, and two desks, one of which was of massive mahogany and must have cost a fortune to rocket up from Earth-side. The other was smaller, of metal and obviously very utilitarian, boasting four phone screens. There were several of the pseudo-windows on the walls, one at least ten feet by six and, unless Bader was mistaken, depicting Mount Etna, as seen from the vicinity of Taormina; the air crystal clear, the sea cobalt, the town a dream Sicilian town, Etna itself topped with unbelievably white snow. He didn't place the other tri-di photos but they too had an aspect of either Southern Italy or Sicily.

There were three occupants of the room. The one behind the metal desk was obviously a secretary and a non-entity. The girl on one of the couches was Gina Angel and she looked at Rex Bader mockingly; she had a tall glass in one hand.

It was the one seated behind the wooden desk that counted. He wore an old fashioned, heavy dark suit, complete with buttoned vest and in spite of the heat of the room, a heavy woolen dressing robe. There were beads of sweat on his forehead but he seemed cold. His face was very old and haggered and his eyelids sagged. Only his brown eyes, which seemed too large for his face, held life.

A thick gray tongue came out and licked shrunken lips. He took two deep breaths of the humid air and got out, "Who sen' you here, Mr. Bader?" He ignored the presence of Al Rich and Rocky.

Rex Bader though about it.

Before he had come up with an answer, the shrunken, sick old man said, "How you like to make twenny-five gran', Mr. Bader, hah?"

Rex said, "Didn't Al tell you? Money means nothing to me. I have an unlimited account in a Swiss bank."

"Don' crack wise with me, you son va bitch."

IX

It came to Rex Bader where he had heard the accent before. He was an inveterate fan of revivals of old-fashioned movies, particularly the classic comedies. Not more than a few weeks before he had laughed his way through Charlie Chaplin's *The Great Dictator*. Jack Oakie had played a burlesque Mussolini and this was the accent he had used. Or perhaps a still better example might be Chico, the Marx borther who pretended to be an Italian. Rex Bader had never heard anyone actually talk in such idiom and had never expected to. It was a bit difficult to take seriously.

Rocky leaned back against the wall and inspected his fingernails. Al Rich went over to the couch on which Gina Angel sat, murmured something to her and took a place at the other end. Gina Angel was evidently inwardly amused about something or other. Today, she wore a Greek revival tunic which made her look several years younger than had the golden sari of the gambling rooms.

Without taking his eyes from Rex Bader, the old man said, "Emanuele. That report, Sophia Anastasis, she justa send up. Only the important parts, hah?"

Emanuele was the colorless one behind the smaller desk. "Yes, sir," he said and took up a sheet of paper. He scanned it and said, "Mr. Bader's home is in New Princeton. His mini-apartment is in one of the older high-rise apartment buildings, on the eighth basement level, among the ultra-markets, garages and so forth, where the rent in minimal. As a young man he studied aviation but was unable to secure employment when almost all aircraft became automated. Later he took additional courses pertaining to the petroleum industry, but was unable to find employment there either."

Rex Bader took a breath and said, "Nuclear power is coming in. Petroleum products going out."

The old man said nothing to that. Emanuele went on. "He took additional courses which led to his being able to apply for and secure a private investigator's license."

"Hah," the old man snorted. "A private eye. A shamus." His large brown eyes ran up and down Rex Bader's figure. "How'sa business, Mr. Bader? It'sa long time since I seen a shamus."

"Not too bad," Rex said.

"How'sa his business, Emanuele?" the old man said, without removing his eyes from Rex Bader.

Emanuele cleared his throat. "Last year, nine months out of the twelve, Mr. Bader applied for and received his Negative Income Tax. The other three months he slightly cleared the applicable poverty level and hence was not eligible for NIT."

Al Rich said gently, "Off hand I would risk a guess that the suit he wears came from Dean's on Bond Street and cost approximately three hundred and fifty pseudo-dollars. The cravat probably came from Martin and Harlow's and cost at least seventy-five."

"Shud up, Al," the old man said without looking at him. "Who sen' you up here, Mr. Bader, hah?" Then, before the other could answer, "How you like to make that twenty-five gran'?"

"I've already got a client. I'm an old Philip Marlow and Travis McGee fan. I couldn't betray a client's trust.

We private eyes have integrity."

"What'sa matter with you, hah? I tol' you not to crack wise. You think maybe Rocky he'sa can't work you over a little, hah?"

Rex Bader looked over at the expressionless Rocky. "Maybe he could, particularly with some help."

Gina Angel laughed softly.

"No help necessary," Rocky said softly, his eyes on Rex Bader's shoes.

"Shud up, Rocky," the old man said. He breathed deeply for long moments, his sallow waxlike skin that of a corpse.

Rex Bader couldn't help but wonder about the extent to which the one quarter gravity assisted in keeping this living mummy alive.

Al Rich said softly, "Over in the orbiting hotel we have some fairly new developments that can break down a mind as efficiently as Miss Beauregard's is being repaired."

"Shud up, Al," the old man said. "You know we don' use rough stuff no more." He shook his head at Rex. "Al, he'sa crazy. He'sa seen too many of them ol' gangster movies. I was justa kid about Rocky."

Rex said, "You couldn't do it anyway. You'd be afraid to. You don't know who sent me here, and why. Anything happen to me, and you'd get landed on like a sky load of bricks—possibly."

The old man breathed very deeply several times, as though all this talk was exhausting him. "Okay, Mr. Bader. You come up, Satellite City for something. Okay, I make a deal, wit' you. You tell me why you come and who sen' you, and I tell you anything you wanta know. We put all the cards ona table."

Rex Bader said, "I came up to find out whether or not

it was possible to commit *any* crime here in Satellite City, if one had sufficient money."

"And you found out," Al Rich said softly. "You can't. The Satellite City Authority is a reputable, high ethical——"

Gina Angel laughed lowly again and Al Rich broke it off to look at her in irritation.

The old man said, "An' who sen you, Mr. Bader, to fin' this thing out?"

Rex Bader said, "The government of the United States of the Americas."

Al Rich said tightly, "What department?"

"The criminal division of the Inter-American Bureau of Investigation."

The old man said, "Thatsa what I was afraid of."

Al Rich said, "Why you? Why a non-government man? Why a private investigator?"

Rex said, "I wouldn't know. Possibly because you people have penetrated the Octagon to the point where government agents would immediately be pinpointed. I'm an unknown. The last of the private eyes, as someone called me in deprecation not too long ago."

The usually so sauve Al Rich said. "So why are you sounding off so nice now? Does the twenty-five thousand pseudo-dollars sound good to you?"

Rex looked at him. "Because there is nothing in my instructions that prevents it. My instructions were to come here and find whether it was possible to buy any crime here, anything at all. How I found out was largely up to me. I opted for murder."

Rich snapped, "And found it was a lot on nonsense."

Rex tilted his head slightly. "Did I? Or was the whole thing a put-up job? How soon was I spotted as a phoney? How long have you really known that I couldn't raise a hundred thousand pseudo-dollars in as many years?"

The old man had been catching up with his breathing. Now he leaned back in his chair and put two clawlike hands on the desk top.

He said, "Al, Rocky, Emanuele; get out. Gina, *tesora mio*, get Mr. Bader a drink." He looked at Rex. "I almos' made a very bad mistake, Mr. Bader, hah? Sit down, hah? We talk it over."

The three men got, Al Rich evidently somewhat surprised, the other two expressionless zombis meant to take orders and who did.

Gina, soft amusement on her perfectly complexioned face, stood and went to the old fashioned bar. She turned to Rex and liften on perfect eyebrow. "Pseudo-whisky and water, wasn't it?"

"That'll be fine. You have a good memory."

"Thank you, kind sir. All gamblers do, you know." She looked at the old man.

He shook his head and brought a handkerchief from an inner pocket and swabbed his forehead and then his neck with it. Rex Bader wondered what was keeping him alive.

She brought the drink, a satisfying amber color and with three very large ice cubes.

He had settled into one of the comfort chairs. Sweat was trickling down his chest in a rivlet to his belly. He couldn't figure out how the girl continued to look cool. How the old man kept from melting down into a puddle, with all these clothes on, he'd never know. The cold drink was, off hand, the best one he had ever enjoyed in his life; he took down half of it in three gulps.

He looked at his host. "Okay. Great. It's your yo-yo, start spinning it."

The old-timer looked at the girl, who had made herself

another drink and settled back into her original spot on the couch. Then he looked at Rex. He said, "Mr. Bader, you ever heard of Nicolo Mangano?"

"I don't think so."

"Gina, *mio caro*, you tell Mr. Bader about Nicolo Mangano, Big Nick." He leaned back in his chair still further and dropped his sagging eyelids and breathed deeply.

The lovely Gina put a finger to lip in thought. "Well, where should we begin?" she said. "Possibly in Palermo on March 30, 1282, during the French occupation of Sicily. The occupation was oppressive to the point that the Sicilians revolted and adopted a slogan *Morte ala Francia Italia anela!* You speak Italian, Mr. Bader?"

"No."

"It means, *Death to the French is Italy's cry!* The initials of the slogan spell *Mafia* and it was by this name that the underground organization became known eventually. It was a patriotic organization, Mr. Bader, but its only recourse is to fight the foe was secret violence and it became very good at this, and continued the struggle for centuries. However, after Garibaldi, Cavour and Mazzini had united Italy and the battle was won, the organization was too steeped in the soil of Sicily—or should we say the blood of the Sicilian people—to disappear. And when large elements of the population immigrated, especially to the United States, that supposed paradise for immigrants, the Mafia organization went with them."

She hesitated for a moment, took up her glass and took a sip. She looked at the old man but his eyes remained closed.

She said, "Have you ever heard of the Black Hand, Mr. Bader?"

"I don't think so."

"Some of the Mafia members—not all—found themselves poverty-stricken in that period before the First World War and turned to what they knew best, terror and extortion. Most of their activities were directed. against fellow Italian immigrants, but not all."

"Nicolo Mangano, Gina," the old murmered.

"Yes. We come now to Big Nick Mangano who was born in the town of Girgenti, somewhere about the turn of the century. By the time he was a young fellow it became obvious that Nicolo was not going to prosper in Sicily. Farming was impossibly bad, there was no work, and there wasn't even enough stealing, extortion and political corruption to stretch out among the *Mafiosi*. His uncle Pasquale had migrated to St. Louis and had become a *capo di diecina*, that is, a chief of ten under the Don there, the local leader of the Mafia. Pasquale did well enough that he was able to send for his nephew, Nick, who found employment opportunities no better in America than they had been in Italy. While still a boy he became a member of the Green Ones, the local branch of the Mafia."

"Not so long, Gina, hah?" the old man said without opening his eyes."

"Very well. When prohibition came along, it was found that cooking alky, as the expression went, paid off better than extortion and overnight the Mafia throughout the country found themselves comparitively prosperous. Gangsters such as Al Capone——"

"Scarface," the old man muttered.

". . . came to the fore. At first there was considerable conflict with the Camorra, a rival secret organization largely from Naples, but in Atlantic City in 1920 the two organizations were united and the term Cosa Nostra was first heard. The gang wars, particularly in Chicago and

New York made it obvious that strong organization had to be insisted upon or soon no one would be left to enjoy the large sums being realized. Such gentlemen . . ." she made a moue ". . . compared to Scarface Al, that is—such gentlemen as Charles Luciano——"

"Lucky," the old man muttered.

". . . and Frank Costello——"

"Son va bitch fink," the old man muttered.

". . . brought comparative order and eliminated a good many of the older group of the tommygun school. But now came Roosevelt and the ending of the lucrative bootlegging era. The Cosa Nostra had to look into new fields. There were prostitution, gambling, armed robbery, kidnapping, extortion again, usury, labor unions and narcotics. But there was also a new element coming along and our Big Nick Mangano was possibly the first to realize the ramifications. By this time he had been married twice and had four sons and two daughters. He sent them all to the best schools to which they could be admitted . . ." she cleared her throat ". . . which weren't too very good, and he saw that they took their degrees, either in law or business. I understand that he had a bit of difficulty with a couple of the boys but in those days Big Nick wasn't called Big Nick without reason. All of them graduated.

"Big Nick was also possibly the first of the Dons to realize that bank robbery and kidnapping were no answer. He was also the first to realize that men, Mafia members or no, such as Dillinger——"

"Hah, Johnny," the old man snorted.

". . . Baby Face Nelson, Pretty Boy Floyd, and such, had to go. They caused to much stink. Indeed, when they got a little *too* mad-dog, it wasn't beyond Big Nick to deny them hideouts or even to, uh, finger them for the FBI or local authorities."

The old man grunted mild rejection of that.

Gina went on. "Prostitution was also soon on the way out. The bordellos of the past melted away along with the old Victorian mores. There just wasn't enough money in it anymore. The corrupt labor unions were lucrative for awhile, but membership in them began to fall off drastically shortly after the Second War. By the end of the Asian War blue collar workers were in a minority and white collar workers seldom joined unions at all, and when they did they wouldn't submit to Mafia control. Gambling was still profitable, especially, surprisingly enough to the really old hands, legal gambling. You could make more in the legitimate casinos of Las Vegas, Reno, or the Bahamas and Cuba, before Castro, than you could operating floating crap tables, or selling policy numbers. Big Nick was one of the first to see this and to put his now extensive resources into the field.

"And by this time a new generation was coming along. Nick's grandchildren went to Ivy League schools and when they graduated, some taking Masters or Doctors degrees, they went into business, politics, some even into the arts and professions, always backed, of course, by Big Nick's money and power, because Nick by now was chief of the American Mafia, or Cosa Nostra, if you will, or The Syndicate, which was a new term coming up.

"By this time, Mr. Bader, the resources of the Syndicate—we'll drop such nasty terms as Mafia, Camorra and Cosa Nostra—were remarkable and Big Nick, once again, was one of the first to realize that the dealing in narcotics must go. It would only result, eventually, in really extensive action on the part of the federal government. Besides, investment in resorts, nightclub chains, restaurant chains and real estate actually in the long run paid off better, pariculary if you made a point of having top politicians protecting your interests.

"And now the fourth generation was coming onto the scene. They, Mr. Bader, were aristocrats by birth. Long since, most of the families had made such changes in their names as from Adamo Moretti to Adam Moore. Most went into business or law, almost invariably associated with Syndicate projects, but not always. However, *all* were available if required. *All*, period. Big Nick made a point of that, and Big Nick's word was final. Along in here, one of his groups acquired the first really large banking chain that was to become part of the Syndicate, a big step upward from the street ursury of early days. And along in here the half dozen or so most important families, from old days, those who had forged ahead, leaving the past behind, divorced themselves from the Mafia of early times. In fact, they were instrumental in its dissolution, when the authorities needed assistance in breaking up the remnants of the old timers."

The old man grunted unhappily at that, but without opening his eyes.

Gina took another sip of her drink and went on. "By this time, Mr. Bader, you have no idea of the resources of the associated families."

"I have some idea," Rex Bader said, just to say something. "I understand that one group, Diversified Industries, bought the Bahama Islands."

"A fairly major transaction, but a profitable one, admittedly. Only Satellite City offers more in the way of freedom. So now, Mr. Bader, we arrive at the fifth generation. Do you know who the richest single person in the world is, Mr. Bader? In this world of ours in which it is so difficult to remain rich, in which the rich are being squeezed out one by one by confiscatory taxes, by revolution, and by dog-eat-dog competition among themselves?"

"I haven't the vaguest idea, Miss Angel."

"I am."

X

The old man opened his eyes, took a deep double breath and sighed. He said, "Gina, she'sa talk a long time. She'sa talk enough. What I wan'a know now, Mr. Bader. You say you a private eye. Okay. What you find out?"

Rex Bader looked at him. "That you're still alive, Big Nick."

The old man nodded. "That'sa right. And what else?"

"That the descendents of the Mafia are too big and too respectable to bother with crime—in the usual sense."

"That'sa right, too. Gina, you tell Mr. Bader, lika you tell me the other day, about the kings and all."

Gina laughed and tucked her long, good legs beneath her on the couch. "Another drink, Mr. Bader?"

He shook his head regretfully. "No thanks, I'm not much of a drinker."

"By the looks of you, you could use a straight mixer. Coke or something."

"I love you," he said.

She swung her legs out, got up and went to the bar and mixed ice and a semi-bitter something evidently based on grapefruit. At least it was cold—and moist.

She said, after she'd returned to her position on the couch, "Nick was referring to such as the Battenbergs."

"Come again?" Rex said, sipping the drink.

"They changed their name to Mountbatten, after becoming British."

He shook his head again.

She said, "They began as a bandit family in Germany and their racket was having a small band of muscle men who extorted tolls from travelling merchants along the roads and along the rivers. After a while they called themselves barons, or some such, and as time passed they became more respectable. And as more time passed, they became still more respectable. And they married into other families with actually the same background, and after a couple of centuries or so some of their descendents became kings in countries like Greece."

Rex said, impatiently, "Okay. Great. What are we getting to?"

"The next generation married into the royal family of England."

He looked at her blankly.

It was her turn to be impatient. "They originated as a bunch of extortionists and would up kings of England. You can't get much higher than being a king of Great Britain."

She said, "Very well. Take your own country. During Prohibition, Big Nick was a small operator compared to a New England financier who practically cornered the market in Scotch. The son of a rather fast-moving Irish immigrant himself, he fathered three United States Senators, one of whom became president. In less than three generations, they had become one of the *royal families* of the country."

"I see what you mean," Rex Bader said. "Somewhere along the line when I was supposedly getting an education, I read that all slaves had a king as their ancestor and that all kings had slaves."

"Right. This is what Big Nick is trying to point out. After a hundred years and more, those who immigrated to America as poverty striken members of an obscure and largely criminal Sicialian secret society, are now some of the most responsible people in the world."

Nicolo Mangano opened his eyes again. Rex Bader wondered how he found the strength.

He said, "Mr. Bader, we wan' no trouble, hah? This is a good operation. We wan' no trouble from the United States, hah? From Common Europe. We wan' no trouble from the Soviet Complex, even, and we do practical no business wit them. Mr. Bader, Satellite City she'sa got no space force. She'sa got no bombs. Thisa city is at everybody's mercy, hah? We'rea tolerated because we'rea handy, hah? Like Switzerland in old days. Hitler, he don' hit Switzerland, hah? Mussolini, he don'. Way back, Napoleon, he'sa guy from Corsica takes everybody. But he'sa no bother Switzerland. How come? On accounta Switzerland is good business. Clearin' house for ever'body, like. That'sa what Satellite City is today, Mr. Bader. Clearin' house."

"All right. Great," Rex said. "I get the message."

Big Nick nodded. It was difficult to conceive of the shriveled little man as once having the size to deserve the nickname. He said, "So you go back to your boss, hah? And you tell him Satellite City is pure legit. We don' cause no trouble wit' nobody."

"Okay," Rex Bader said, coming to his feet. "I'll tell them you said so. One thing. I don't know how you handle your Bourse, your orbital hospital and your science wheel. Profitably, I assume. However, your boy Al Rich and whoever else works with him on it, such as Senor Byass in Tangier, go a little too far in promoting this come-on that you can get literally anything in Satellite City."

"Al he'sa in charge of the orbital hotel. He'sa always make a good profit."

"I'll bet. It's a well done resort, for those who can afford it, and such items as all out gambling will cause no heat down Earth-side, but spread the word that you can get anything up here, including the thrill of murdering girls, and sooner or later you're going to be in major trouble—as witness my being here to check."

Big Nick looked thoughtful and swabbed his head with a fresh handkerchief. He nodded. "That Al, he'sa too ambitious hah? Satellite City she'sa too big an operation to mess wit' peanuts. Big Nick he'sa take care of it, Mr. Bader. Now, how you wan' your twenny-five gran'?"

Rex Bader shook his head. "No matter how you turned it over to me, they'd find out. They'd probably confiscate it. Even if they didn't, the fact that I'd taken it would cast reflections on my report of what I fould in Satellite City—and you'd get nothing for your money. I made a little in the casino last night." He nodded at Gina Angel. "Thanks to Miss Angel. I'll consider that my bonus."

She looked at him dryly. "You mean you really do have integrity?"

"A little, perhaps. Or maybe it's just that this is one of the few really good assignments I've ever had. I'd like to keep my reputation with those that hired me. In the long run, it might be more profitable than trying to hang onto Mr. Mangano's present."

She stood too. Nicolo Mangano closed his eyes again. Evidently, so far as he was concerned, the interview was over.

Gina Angel saw Bader to the door.

He looked at her from the side of his eyes. "You mean they've put the whole thing in your name?"

"That's right."

"Well, why?"

"Various reasons, legal and others. It has to be in somebody's name." She grimaced in a sort of self-deprecation. "Somebody who can be trusted and somebody who never leaves Satellite City any more." She made a face at him. "Not even to hunt tiger."

"Why would that be?"

"No legal papers can be served up here, Mr. Bader. No Earth-side laws apply. No nation has jurisdiction. Not even the Reunited Nations has any jurisdiction. But off-hand I can think of a few, if any, countries of importance Earth-side that wouldn't have lawyers, revenue men and what not pouncing the moment that I sat foot on their soil. It's simpler to have the whole thing in one name. Then, only I am an exile in Satellite City. The others can come and go."

He made an attempt at the light. "So you own Satellite City? Will you marry me."

She grinned at him. "Nope. And nobody else that isn't a member of one of the old families. We haven't got *that* far away from the days of Scarface Al. Do you want two or three more holes in the head?"

"Not especially," he said, very earnestly.

She opened the door and let him out.

Al Rich was there, the always present Rocky, and the thin man with the disagreeable face who was obviously Big Nick's ultimate bodyguard and even shook down such Satellite City's bigwigs as Al Rich, before they entered the presence. The latter ignored Rex Bader.

Al Rich said smoothly, "Finish your business with Mr. Mangano?"

Rex started for the elevator, walking carefully in the one quarter gravity. It was the damnedest thing. "I suppose so. When's the next passenger transport down Earth-side, Rich?"

Al Rich and Rocky accompanied him. "Tomorrow morning. Nine o'clock. Plan to be on it?"

"I suppose so. I've done everything I was sent to do, and that supposed unlimited bank account isn't all that unlimited. I'll have to account for everything I spend."

For the first time since they had met, the suave Al Rich allowed a slightly supersilious expression on his face. "Our way of life is a bit too rich for a private investigator who's usually on Negative Income Tax, ah?"

Rex Bader didn't bother to react. "Much too rich," he said. "I can find my own way."

"We'll come along," Rich said. "I had a couple of things I wanted to talk to you about."

They returned to Rex Bader's apartment. He sank onto the living room couch. Al Rich took one of the comfort chairs and Rocky leaned against the wall, checking his manicure. It was an excellent manicure; evidently, even the heavies in Satellite City must be turned out like the ultimate in gentlemen.

Rex Bader said, "It's your canoe, start paddling it."

The other looked at him pensively. "What did the old man have to say to you, Bader?"

For some reason, Rex Bader was feeling perverse. Possibly, it was the other's attitude. No longer was he the honored guest.

"He told me that Satellite City was, as he put it, strictly legit, and wanted no trouble."

"I already told you that. What else did you learn?"

"Various items, such as the fact that the whole project is evidently legally—if that term makes sense up here—

in the name of Miss Angel, which is mildly surprising, but I'm not exactly up on international property laws, not to speak of whatever ones they might have that apply to space."

The other's eyes narrowed. "Oh, you did, ah? You were in there a long time. What else did Big Nick blab about?"

Rex Bader looked at him in amusement. "I'll just bet he'd love to hear that term, coming from you."

Rich continued to stare at him. "Come on, what else?"

"Look Rich, I'm still a guest in this spinning top. I've paid my way. I don't think I like your attitude."

"That's too bad. The hundred thousand pseudo-dollars you used to sneak in here will be refunded to your account in the Grundbank. Big Nick's orders. Such other expenses as you've run up will be deducted from the sum you won in the gambling rooms last night. Your trip's on the house, Bader. So you're not exactly a bona-fide guest. Talk up. What else did the old man say?"

"I don't think I'll tell you."

Al Rich snapped, "Rocky! Take him!"

The heavy-set man came in with deceptive speed, the seeming laziness gone out of him. Rex Bader hardly had time to come to his feet. He tried to slip to one side to avoid the rush. Had the other hit him with that first punch, the fight would have been over then and there—which might have been for the best in the long run.

Rex Bader barely got his left arm up in time. Rocky's large cement-hard fist numbed his arm. He turned from the expected knee and it caught him on the thigh, knocking him back against the wall.

Al Rich sat there and watched, a slight amusement on his face.

Rocky rushed in again, foiling Rex Bader's attempt to

bob by catching him on the forehead with a wild swing. He wasn't as highly trained a pug as all that, evidently. Rex hit him as hard and as fast as he could, three blows to the face, left, right, left. He put everything he had into the last one. He had hit men that hard before and always they had gone down. But Rocky rushed him again and Rex Bader backed up fast, trying to get to the room's center where he could better operate.

Rocky came in lithely, with the deceptive grace that Rex had already noted. Rex circled him slowly. He hit the stocky man twice more, but not as hard. He was trying to stay away from the other who had now fallen into more of a wrestler's, or, karate expert's, stance. He did not try to hit back. At the second blow his fingers slipped off the wrist of Rex Bader before he could get sufficiently good a grip for whatever he had in mind.

Discretion told Rex Bader to try to escape from the room, but he couldn't run from a man, particularly when Al Rich still sat there, sardonically watching.

Rocky dived for Rex Bader's legs. The other avoided him by inches, and slipped sideward. Rocky rolled, but by the time he had come to his feet, Bader had slipped behind him, brought his two hands together and chopped them down on the back of his opponent's neck with as much strength as he could still master. The pace was exhausting him, and the drinks he had had weren't helping his reflexes.

He had expected his opponent to go down, but Rocky whirled with that special agility of his and Bader was too off balance to retreat quickly enough. Rocky snagged an arm and began to pull the smaller man toward him. Rex Bader hit him three times about the nose and mouth, but slowly Rocky pulled him closer, locking his arms about the waist, fists in the small of the other's back, his shoulders pressing against Rex Bader's throat.

They stood there motionless for a long moment, and then the professional bodyguard began to squeeze. Rex Bader could feel the creaking of his rib cage under the pressure. The lights in the room began to go darker, he could feel the air whooshing from his lungs. He knew suddenly that Rocky was perfectly capable of breaking his spine.

Al Rich said softly, "All right, Rocky. That's enough of a lesson for one session."

He could feel the pressure fall away and tried to shake his head for clarity, but his body failed him. Black fog rolled in and Rex Bader collapsed to the floor. He didn't hear the others go.

XI

He awoke sometime in the night, figuring night as they did in Satellite City, that is between the hours of 9 p.m. and 6 a.m., Greenwich Meridian time. He was stiff and sore, his clothes a rumpled mess. He couldn't remember ever having taken such a beating before.

He found his way to the bathroom, agonized out of his clothes and got under the shower. He took as much heat as he could, stood there a long time. Finally he got out and dried himself and stumbled his way to the bedroom. He didn't bother with pajamas, but slumped nude into the softness, pulled the bedcover over him and was asleep.

Happily, he awoke early enough not to miss the shuttlecraft that was to take whatever guests were scheduled to return Earth-side over to the space dock. He still ached brutally and wondered whether Rocky had broken any of his ribs. He felt them gingerly. So far as he could tell, they were all right.

He packed what there was to be packed, including the dress shoes and evening shirt he had ordered for the Galaxy Room the night before last. He didn't have room for the suit, or he would have taken that as well. The hell with them and their little rackets for picking up every last buck from their clientele. The shoes would have cost at least a hundred psuedo-dollars in any swank Earth-side shop.

He left the bags in the delivery closet and then, remembering the warning of the stewardess down in Beni-Abbes, made a last call on the bathroom. He also drank two glasses of water, but couldn't bring himself to breakfast.

He left the suite and made his way to the reception hall and to the bright young thing there. He was beginning to detest all the bright young things in Satellite City.

He said, "My name's Harold Brown. I'd like to return Earth-side. Could I have an accounting of my bill?"

Her smile told him that his slightest wish was her command. She flicked a switch on one of her phone screens and murmured something into it and looked up into his face again, almost immediately. "You have a balance of 3,450 psuedo-dollars, Mr. Brown, would you like that to be deposited to your account in the Grundbank in Geneva?"

"No, I wouldn't."

"Oh, of course. You would like it distributed to the personnel who served you during your stay, in the way of gratuity?"

He all but snarled at that one. "No, I wouldn't. I want it deposited to the account of Rex Bader in the National Data Banks of the United States."

She held onto her smile, but barely, and said, "Certainly, Mr. Brown. Your shuttlecraft leaves very shortly, from Airlock Two, right over there."

He went over to the Protective offices and secured his gyro-jet pistol from an Antony Berch who looked at his marked face questioningly, but said nothing untoward.

His return to the space dock was a duplication of his journey to the orbital hotel only two days previously.

Was it only two days he had spent in Satellite City? Right now, it seemed like a couple of weeks.

And in most respects the return to the spaceport at Beni-Abbes was a duplication of the trip up, with the exception, of course, that they were a fraction of the size of the rocket transporter and no airborne booster craft was involved when earth atmosphere was reached. After the pilot of their craft had retarded their speed with rocket blasts several times, wings emerged from the sides of their now airplane and they came in for a standard landing on wheels, as though they were a glider.

He made quick arrangements for a flight to Algiers and as soon as he was settled in the jetplane, brought forth his pocketphone.

He opened it and said into the small screen, "The United States of the Americas." Then, "Greater Washington." Then, "John Mickoff, Inter-American Bureau of Investigation, at the Octagon."

When John Mickoff's face faded in, he was scowling.

"Bader here," Bader growled.

"You mean Brown, don't you? And what are you calling me for? And where are you?"

"I mean Bader and I'm on my way first to Algiers where I'll pick up a plane for the States. What're my orders?"

"Wait a minute, damn it," Mickoff said and evidently flicked on another phone. He returned shortly and said, "I'll contact you at your apartment, in the morning." He was a man of approximately Rex Bader's own age and able to project an air of both being easy going and alert. He was right now, however, far from pleased.

Rex Bader grunted and switched off the phone.

There was no direct flight between Algiers and

Greater Washington. He had to make connections through Lisbon. The effects of the beating were beginning to wear off sufficiently to the point that he accepted the lunch offered as they crossed the Mediterranean to the Iberian peninsula and the areas once known as Spain and Portugal, now both part of Common Europe.

At Lisbon, he took a shuttle-copter to the Western European jetport, anchored some fifteen miles off the coast and from there the Supersonic to the American International Jetport, twenty miles off Long Beach. Once again, a shuttle-copter took him to the mainland.

A public bus would have been cheaper, but he was still on the expense account and still feeling like he had been put through a wringer. At the terminal he summoned an individual electro-steamer to take him to New Princeton.

He disembarked from the vehicle in the transportation station of his building and immediately took the elevator for the eighth basement floor. He had left his luggage at the jetport. It ought to be here by now.

The identity screen picked him up and the door of his mini-apartment opened up.

He stepped into the tiny apartment and looked about in self reproof. After the ultra-luxury of his stay in Tangier, and especially of his Satellite City spree, the drabness of the reality of his life came doubly home to him. Given success on this job, he might have looked forward to other assignments, but he had a sneaking suspicion that it wasn't going to be considered a success. At the very most, it was partial.

His baggage hadn't arrived in the delivery box, as yet. He shrugged. There was no hurry. He went into the little dining nook, sat down at the auto-table and dialed a sparse evening meal. He was going to have to get back

114

into the habit of eating synthetics and such proletarian fare.

In the morning, the humming of the phone screen on the stand next to his bed awakened him.

The face of John Mickoff was there. He said, "You still in bed, Bader?"

"No, I'm chinning myself on the damn chandelier."

"The Chief says come down soonest." Mickoff grinned at him. "I've been looking at some of your swindle sheets. You didn't think the department's going to clear some of those expenses, do you? Younger brother, those clothes you bought in London. That money you tossed around in Tangier."

Even as he swung his legs around to the floor, Bader growled back, "They wanted me to portray the kind of character that'd be able to fritter away a hundred thousand for a thrill. What did you expect me to do, wear a breechcloth and eat synthetic ham sandwiches?"

Mickoff said, "Younger brother, why can't I get assignments like that? Living it up in Satellite City."

"You don't have the I.Q.," Bader told him and snapped the phone off.

He went through the routine of removing his beard with depilatory shaving cream, of showering, dressing and breakfast delivered to his autotable from the ultramation kitchens several floors below him.

Greater Washington was about five hundred kilometers south. He'd better be on his way. The new chief of the Inter-American Bureau of Investigation was trying to prove himself by putting on a veneer of toughness and Rex Bader had a suspicion that he wasn't going to be ecstatic about Rex Bader.

He went down the two floors to the transport station, walked over to the metro entry and took the first mini-bus to New Princeton's central terminal. He switched there to a twenty-seater express to Greater Washington which took them at a good five hundred or six hundred kilometer clip through the automated underground ultra-highways.

At the Greater Washington Terminal he took a mini-bus to the Octagon and went through the usual routine of having to clear himself, state his appointment, and the rest of it, through his pocket phone cum identity card. He had been through all this before. The appointment was confirmed. They checked you out, these days, kilometers before you ever got near enough to take a shot at a bigwig—if that was your intention.

At the Octagon Terminal, he stated his business all over again to the screen on one of the reception desks and in moments there was a two-place floater there to take him to his destination which was several kilometers off through corridors and up and down ramps.

He was becoming reasonably familiar with the route. They finally pulled up in a side corridor before a door which immediately slid open on his approach. The office beyond contained a single desk.

John Mickoff got up and came around to shake hands. "Who socked you?" he said.

"The last of the hoods."

"I thought you knew how to take care of yourself."

"So did I but I don't. Not well enough. Next time I hope you can go around and around with him, instead of me. Hooligan expecting me?"

That's pronounced Harrigan, old chum. Preferably, Mr. Harrigan, as you'll probably soon find out." John Mickoff grinned at him. "But, yep, he said to bring you in as soon as you arrived. I'll keep my fingers crossed for you."

He led the way to an inner door and stood there before the identity screen. He said, "Bader, sir."

"That's Mr. Bader," Rex muttered to him.

"Huh," Mickoff murmured back, under his breath.

The door opened and they entered. Rex had been here before and was mildly surprised that Howard Harrigan, who had just recently taken over the job, had made so few changes. Possibly, it was because the place was all but an institution to the American people. There had been many a fire-side chat type speech from this Spartan room, usually dark speeches on the threat of subversion emanating from the Soviet Complex or China. Harrigan didn't beat the drum to quite the extent his predecessor had, possibly because it had been beaten so long that nobody was interested in listening. Nowadays, the Soviet Complex was just about as interested in subverting the West as the West was in subverting the Soviet Complex. Time had taken the chill from the Cold War.

It might have warmed up the Cold War but not even time had warmed up Howard Harrigan. He was a frosty man who looked quite a bit like photos Rex Bader had seen of Grover Cleveland. And, it came to him now, how many politicians seemed to look like Grover Cleveland; possibly voters didn't trend toward thin men. It had never occured to him before how many politicians, down through the years, were at least well rounded.

Howard Harrigan didn't offer to shake hands. He said coldly, "Good morning, Bader."

Bader said, "Good morning, sir." He took one of the three chairs that sat before the other's desk, without invitation, and crossed his legs. He was beginning to build up a defensive irritation.

John Mickoff took one of the other chairs and a note pad and stylus from his pockets.

Harrigan said, "No notes will be necessary, John."

"Yes, sir." Mickoff returned the pad to his pocket.

Harrigan looked at Rex Bader. "So you blew your cover."

Bader made with his slight rueful smile. "No, sir. I never had any."

The director of what amounted to all the United States of the Americas' police, secret police, espionage and counter-espionage forces glared at him. "I had good men work for weeks on that cover we supplied you. Evidently, it didn't last for more than a few hours, once you were on your own."

"No, sir. I'm not saying the boys didn't do as good a job as they could. They must have taken every measure to blot me out of the National Data Banks and the International Data Banks. And they did a beautiful job with the banking deal in Switzerland. The trouble is this, The Syndicate—if that term makes any sense any more; possibly The Corporation would be better—evidently has a computer data bank of its own, geared to their special needs. Oh, they knew all about me by the time I got up to Satellite City. Maybe they were puzzled a little, and were intrigued with what I was up to and who I was working for, but they knew me, all right, all right."

Harrigan picked up a pipe and a tobacco pouch, leaned back in his old-time swivel chair and said, "Very well. A complete report." He stuffed the pipe and lit it.

Rex Bader gave it to him, including the twenty-five thousand pseudo-dollars which he had turned down.

John Mickoff had chuckled at that, and Harrigan had silenced him with a glare.

When Bader had completely finished, Harrigan thought about it for awhile and then said, "And what is your own opinion?"

Rex shrugged. "I think that substantially they're telling the truth. There is nothing they want less than to draw the enmity of our own government, Common Europe, or even the Soviet Complex. They want to remain as legal as is necessary to allow their operation, as they call it, to continue. Al Rich——"

"That would be Alphonse Richetti, sir," Mickoff put in.

". . . is a bit on the impetuous side and so anxious to build up an ultra-wealthy, playboy type clientele that he goes overboard in getting around the idea that anything goes in Satellite City. I think that Mangano will crack down on him, after this."

"You say that this Richetti had you assaulted?"

"He seems to have a bit of the throwback to the old days. There also seems to be some inter-organizational conflict, as in any other big organization, and I get the impression that Al Rich is ambitious. He must be as thwarted as all hell that the whole city is legally in the name of Miss Angel—"

"That would be Gina Angelo, sir," Mickoff said. "Her great grandfather was a Don of one of the early families."

"I got the feeling, I don't know why, that several of her great grandfathers were big wigs in the original Cosa Nostra," Rex said.

Howard Harrigan thought about it for a long time, the other two keeping their peace.

Finally he leaned forward and activated a screen on his desk. He said, "You gentlemen have heard all this?"

A voice said, "Yes."

"Would you like to confront Mr. Bader?"

"A moment," the voice said.

It took considerably longer than a moment, but then the voice said, "Yes, we would."

XII

Mystified, Rex Bader stood and followed the police head through a back door. John Mickoff brought up the rear. On the other side was a room somewhat larger than the office from which they had just emerged, and less austere. It was obviously a conference room, containing little more than a heavy rectangular table and the appropriate chairs about it. There were eight men, of varying ages, and all looked at him in interest when he entered.

They had the air of men who made decisions, who held power, who were used to having their orders obeyed. Rex Bader knew only one, personally, and was surprised to find him in the gathering. It was Colonel Ilya Simonov of the *Chrezvychainaya Komissiya* of the Soviet Complex, an organization that had supposedly been folded many decades previously—and hadn't. The stony eyed colonel, Rex Bader knew, held the Hero's Combat Award, possibly the most difficult decoration to win in the world, and he had earned it—the hard way.

He recognized one more face, among the others. It was that of the Ambassador to the United States of the Americas from Common Europe, Professor Andrew Wilkonson, a tall, slim, semi-bald and very distinguished British economist who had made his mark in the laying out of the present socioeconomic system that applied in what was once called the Old World.

Ilya Simonov nodded to Bader but didn't speak. Rex

nodded back and took the chair Harrigan indicated at the table. Harrigan sat at the table's head and John Mickoff, keeping in the background, took a chair behind and to the left of his chief. He fished out his notebook again but Harrigan, without bothering to turn and look at his assistant, said, "No notes, John."

He looked about the table. "Very well. This, of course, is Mr. Rex Bader, the private investigator we sent to make a preliminary reconnaisance of Satellite City, and to find evidence, if possible, which would put us in a position to take action against that Authority. To a certain extent he failed, since we cannot know to what degree they adapted their real policies when they discovered him to be a plant. However, in other respects, he succeeded."

A gray-faced, gray-suited man with an accent that immediately branded him Teutonic said testily, "In what manner did he succeed? To me it seemed he was most the amateur."

Harrigan looked at him. "He penetrated Satellite City, remained there for two days, saw considerable of the layout, and contacted several of the powers that be. We did not even know that Nicolo Mangano was still alive. Our last report on him is nearly half a century old at which time he was released from federal prison where he had been serving a term for income tax evasion. I might mention, in passing, that his release came from a pardon. It was the only occasion in his career that Mangano ever served time and it only two years, although the sentence was ten. It is not the first time that high ranking elements in The Syndicate have received pardons. Lucky Luciano, as they called him, was serving life when he was pardoned out of a clear sky and the pardon came from the then governor, the very man who had prosecuted him.

"But in this case, the pardon had to emanate from the higher echelons of the Federal government. I mention this in passing, as an indication of the powers wielded by the element now in control of Satellite City."

One of the others, another unknown to Rex Bader, said impatiently, "I cannot see why we do not take united measures against this festering sore. It brings chaos to international banking and securities exchange, and is, from Bader's report, the hideout of the most corrupt and most successful gang of thieves the world has ever seen."

Still another said, very quietly, "I have taken various degrees in international law, but I would hate the job of having to prove in any court, in any country, that any present member of the so-called Syndicate is a criminal. In the first place, I doubt if any of them are; and in the second place I shudder at the thought of the legal weight they could bring to bear."

All eyes were on him, some in obvious disagreement.

He said, wearily, "Let us review the history of Satellite City. It's origins were in the early 1970s not long after the initial moon landings. Utilizing the equipment designed for the Apollo program, it consisted of taking an empty Saturn 5 rocket third stage, removing its engine and turning the inside of its hydrogen fuel tank into a laboratory and living quarters, about the size of a two bedroom apartment in all. It was launched, unmanned, into earth orbit by a two-stage Saturn 5. A day later, three astronauts, launched in an Apollo command ship by a Saturn 1B, rendezvoused and linked up with the space station. They spent four weeks there. After completing their tour in orbit they flew their Apollo back to Earth and shortly after another group came up and stayed for eight weeks, not only conducting scientific experiments but also welding new elements to the infant space station. That was the beginning.

"In those days, there was great controversy among the authorities as to which was most practical, a space station, or platform, or a major base on the moon. Perhaps the moon advocates were correct, considering the fact that Luna had her own raw materials and endless area in which to operate, but billions were spent on the space platform before it was decided to concentrate all future funds on Luna City. Wheels had been developed so that gravity could be maintained; shuttle craft to bring freight and passengers from earth had reached a high efficiency; great spaceport facilities such as those at Beni-Abbes had been created; whole factories had been built in various countries to construct the materials that went into what is now called Satellite City.

"It was a dilemma. What to do with it all? There was too much involved simply to scrap it. And it was then that the Satellite City Authority announced its existence. The roster of names that backed the program was most impressive; hundreds of prominent scientists, hundreds of noted politicians, a score or more of the largest cosmo-corps, multi-national industrial, communications and transportation combines, and literally millions of ordinary citizens who signed petitions. The program? To turn Satellite City, as it was already being called, over to a private corporation to be continued as an orbiting science wheel, an orbiting hospital and, eventually, an orbiting resort hotel. The price? One pseudo-dollar."

For the first time since he had joined this prestigious conference, Rex Bader spoke up. He blurted, "One pseudo-dollar!"

The speaker turned in his direction and nodded. "A little known fact, but it is correct. Nobody seemed at the time to realize that the numerous conglomerates that were supposed to have a share in the Satellite City Authority were all either controlled by The Syndicate, or their holdings were so small as to be meaningless. Within the year, all other elements had been bought out or released their holdings voluntarily. Please recall, that it was not only Satellite City that was involved but for all practical purposes all the shuttle craft, all the spaceport facilities, practically all the factories. I don't believe it has ever been estimated the full value of what was involved in that one pseudo-dollar transaction.

"Of course, at first it was thought that the science wheel and the orbiting hospital would be the major items, and that largely the Satellite City Authority was a philanthropical international organization which would most likely be hard put not to go broke. The orbiting resort hotel was a minor matter, supposedly. However, in short order the Authority had a banking system going, unrestricted by the laws of any earth nation. Next came the Satellite City Bourse, which has become somewhat of a thorn in the side of every stock exchange on Earth. Then came the unrestricted, untaxed, gambling facilities and on and on."

The one who had called for united measures to cut out the festering sore said, "I fail to see the point in this lengthy lecture on a subject with which we are quite familiar."

And the one who had proclaimed himself an international law authority shook his head in reproof. "The point is, my dear sir, that the only possible manner in which the Syndicate could have come in control of anything as overwhelmingly large as the Satellite City Authority was through the chicanery, is you will, of literally hundreds of powerful persons, including many scientists of the highest reputation. But also politicians, up to and including heads of State, some of whom were made fools of, admittedly, but some of whom knew perfectly well what was involved. More important still were the super-corporations, the international corporations that gave the project their support. Do you realize that as little as five percent ownership of stock can control a corporation? The vairous branches of the Syndicate control many corporations, either directly or through persons beholden to them."

"I still fail to see your point!"

"The point is that the elements that own Satellite City still maintain this leverage of theirs. As an authority, in all modesty, in international law, I do not believe it possible for us to apply pressure to Satellite City. Do not forget that some wonderful scientific breakthroughs have been made in the science wheel and their excellence handled publicity almost daily predicts still greater ones. Do not forget that great cures have been achieved in the orbiting hospital. Do not forget, above all, that the political figures under the thumb of The Syndicate are still under the thumb, possibly more so today, since the Authority has proven such a great success financially."

All sank into quiet thought.

Colonel Ilya Simonov said gently, "Then we are powerless?"

Harrigan looked at him impatiently. "That is what we are here to find out, Colonel."

Rex Bader found the courage to speak up again. He said, "Look, gentlemen, so far I fail to see what this has got to do with me. All I was hired to do was go up and find out if they were so far out that you could pay them to do, actually, anything, if you had enough money. Evidently if this proved to be true, you would have felt that you were in a position to move in on them, that the world would have accepted the necessity. Well, maybe I'm wrong, but I came to the conclusion that was a lot of nonsense. They're out for as many quick bucks as they can get, but they aren't stupid."

Harrigan was human enough to sigh. He looked at Ambassador Wilkonson and said, "Professor, could we have a brief on the situation that has brought we of the United States of the Americas, Common Europe and the Soviet Complex together in secret conclave?"

The Ambassador turned to Bader. "Young man, politicians have conducted themselves as though the status quo was changeless. However, there is nothing more changeable than politico-economic systems and the rate of change in the modern world has been accelerating as rapidly as have many other institutions, sciences and so forth. Today, more enlightened than governing groups in the past, we try to control it."

He looked about the table, as though acknowledging the presence of all the rest. "The world, at present is divided into roughly four groups, the United States of the Americas, which does, of course, not as yet include all the nations of the two hemispheres; Common Europe; the Soviet Complex; and the so-called neutral nations. Of these last, only Japan is an advanced industrialized nation, all the others are developing, or emerging countries.

"Our world is in a delicate condition of balance, and at this point none of us represented here this morning wish to disturb that balance. For instance, the Soviet Complex would dislike anything to happen to upset the present government of the United States, because then things would be, ah, up for grabs, to use your Yankee idiom, and the repercussions might eventually disturb the institutions of the Soviet Complex."

"And the same applies the other way around," Harrigan said frostily.

Ilya Simonov nodded. "Of course."

The Ambassador went on. "And Common Europe would hate to see anything happen to the internal conditions applying in either the United States or the Soviet Complex."

"So," Bader said, "like the politicians for donkey's years, to use the Britishism, you wish to continue the status quo."

The Ambassador said wryly, "Jolly good. At least for the time being. At least until we have gotten through the current condition of flux. So you see, if one of the major developing countries such as India or Brazil, were to overthrow their existing government and desire to join forces with any of we three major powers, the balance might be bloody well disturbed."

What in the devil has all this got to do with me?" Bader said in puzzlement.

Harrigan looked at Ilya Simonov. "Colonel?"

Simonov took the ball. "Have you ever heard of Ché-Djilas?"

"Vaguely," Bader said. A radical who has been active in several countries, once or twice successfully. A big mystery man. Always works behind the scenes. Some people don't even believe he exists."

"He exists," the Colonel said grimly. "And his prestige continues to grow. Largely through his efforts, the governments of two of the smaller neutral nations have been overthrown. How long it will be before he is successful in the larger ones is hard to say. We wish to nail him, Bader, before he gets any further. The Ambassador is correct, none of the three world powers want the balance to be disturbed at this stage in history."

Bader was staring at him. "You mean even the Soviet Complex doesn't want these revolts that Djilas is trying to stir up?"

"It most certainly doesn't. It doesn't wish *anything* to happen that might revive the so-called Cold War. There are internal problems enough, not to wish international ones. But to go back to Ché Djilas. The name is a pseudonym made up from those of two revolutionaries of the past. We have no record of his real identity, nor do we even know for certain if Ché is a man or woman. In fact practically all we do know about Ché Djilas is that he is at present in Satellite City."

Rex Bader stared at him still. "I'm beginning to see light and I don't like it. I was happier in the dark."

Harrigan said, "Bader, your first mission didn't work out. You failed to get information that would have given us an excuse to move in on Satellite City, capturing this Djilas and solving other problems as well. Your second mission is to return to Satellite City and arrest, or liquidate, this troublemaker."

XIII

Rex Bader came to his feet. He hissed softly between his teeth and said, "Do I look as though I am completely around the bend?"

The gray faced Teuton said, "A dozen nations have prices on his head, dead or alive. I would imagine the total must be nearly a quarter of a million Common Europe mark-francs which are, of course, on a par with the pseudo-dollar." He added, "The sums are all tax free."

Bader glared at him. "What good is a quarter of a million bucks, if you're dead?"

Ilya Simonov said blandly, "We know he's in Satellite City because one of my men planted an electronic bug on him, in Djakarta. Less than half an hour later, the agent was shot to death but not before being able to report the bug to me. We traced Che Djilas to Satellite City through it, but there evidently the bug was detected and destroyed."

Bader turned his glare in that direction. "Okay. Great. Do you know what that means? It means that the authorities in Satellite City are deliberately protecting him. He didn't have a mop of his own, or he would have found the bug himself, earlier. They found it for him with their sophisticated mops. Ergo, they're protecting him."

"That would seem correct," Simonov nodded.

Bader swept the table with his eyes, still unbelieving of the proposition. He said, "Damn it, my cover was blown. They *know* me. There are no extradition laws in Satellite City. If they allowed me to walk in, arrest this character and take him back to Earth, then a couple hundred of their high paying guests would get the willies. They can't *afford* to allow anybody to be arrested in Satellite City!

"This is stupid. In the first place, they wouldn't allow me to get as far as into the spaceport in Beni-Abbes, not to speak of ever entering the orbital hotel again. But suppose I did get there?" He glared at Ilya Simonov. "Nobody has ever seen this Ché Djilas; seen him and lived, at least. How am I supposed to identify him, even if I did get inside Satellite City again?"

Ilya Simonov twisted his mouth in sardonic amusement. "Frankly, as the expression goes, I don't think you have a chance of an icicle in hell. But we're reaching for straws. He's there. We have him placed. And you are the only agent your government has ever been able to get into Satellite City."

Rex Bader looked back at Howard Harrigan. "Well, it's no use continuing the debate. It's no go. I was practically thrown out of Satellite City after undergoing a beating by an expert. I have no intention of going back."

Harrigan said testily, "We are not without resources. There are such things as plastic surgery, even the altering of your fingerprints."

Bader said, "You spent weeks on establishing my cover last time. How long did it last? These people have been playing cloak and dagger since the 13th Century, before America was discovered." He added nastily, "They figure you're amateurs."

Harrigan said, "John, see Mr. Bader out."

John Mickoff said, "Yes, sir," and came to his feet. As soon as none of those about the table could see his expression, he grinned at Rex Bader and winked.

Mickoff closed the door to the conference room behind them, after they had entered the office of Howard Harrigan.

He said to Rex, "Yellow, eh, younger brother?"

Rex growled nastily, "Don't be an idiot. Can you see me going up there with a neat little arrest warrant and saying to Al Rich, 'Deliver Ché Djilas, or whatever his name is, to me.'? If these characters want this elusive trouble maker so badly, why don't they send some of their military outfits after him?"

Mickoff grinned at him again, even as he led the way to his outer office and the corridor beyond. "You heard the reason. Their own top politicians wouldn't allow them to. The Syndicate has too many of them in their pocket. Yep, I'll bet this meeting was held without the knowledge of the governments involved, with the exception of the Soviet Complex. I doubt if the Syndicate has any members in the Kremlin."

"I wouldn't bet on it," Rex grumbled, even as Mickoff saw him into the hall and summoned a two-seater floater for him. "See you, John."

John Mickoff laughed lightly. "I doubt it, younger brother. I doubt if you'll ever get another assignment through the government. This department or any other. Good luck, Rex. I don't blame you, but a quarter of a million is one hell of a lot of money."

"And one extra hole in the head is one too many," Rex said sourly.

He arrived home in New Princeton in a state of irritation. A quarter of a million pseudo-dollars. Tax free, yet.

Society had gotten to the point, in the advanced countries at least, where nobody starved, went cold or unsheltered nor without proper medical attention. But those who were born without assets found them all but impossible to acquire, taxes being what they were. And those born with them had to dodge, twist and duck to retain them, and every year the ways of evading taxation became more difficult.

Once again, his mini-apartment irritated him. Was he never going to get to the point where he could afford more spacious quarters? He hated doing all his reading on library booster screens from the National Data Banks. He would have loved to have enough room for library shelves and to collect those old books that really appealed to him. He would have loved to have enough wall space to hang a few paintings or prints.

Although it was still early in the day, he had begun to make a bee-line for his little autobar, but then stopped off and flicked on his phone to check mail or messages.

There was only one message. It read:

Cocktails with Miss Sophia Anastasis. Six o'clock. The International Diversified Industries Building, Manhattan.

He stared down at it. Miss Mafia herself. His past relationship with her had not been the happiest. How was it that whenever he came in contact with these people he concluded by being beaten up?

He decided to ignore it.

He could just see himself at a cocktail party thrown by Sophia Anastasis. The waiters probably carried blackjacks. He could still feel the bruised arm where Rocky had slugged him, not to speak of aching ribs.

Then he decided not to. Ignore it, that is.

He was supposedly a private investigator. Did he expect to go through life with nothing more drastic than securing grounds for divorce? Hell, there were no divorces any more, for all practical purposes. Who bothered to get married? And, if they did, what were the complications about getting divorced. Who cared?

Six o'clock. He had time for lunch, a nap, and leisurely preparation for the party. It took only minutes to get to Manhattan from New Princeton by ultra-mated underground highway.

But it wasn't a party. It was a tête-à-tête affair; only he and Miss Anastasis. And cocktails turned out to be champagne. He didn't particularly like bubbly wine, but that was how the ball bounced.

Getting in to see Miss Sohpia Anastasis wasn't as simple as all that. He passed at least three checking points, possibly more. He had no way of knowing how many mini-identity screens rigged to the building's computers might have checked him along the way. But he was first required to identify himself at a reception desk in the metro station of the International Diversified Industries Building, complete to putting his pocket phone-identity card in a slot there. The phone screen on the reception desk said emotionlessly, "You are expected, Mr. Bader. Please take elevator seven to the lobby."

In the lobby, several stories up, he was checked again at a bank of automated reception desks. It might have been the lobby of any business housing the home offices of one of the largest conglomerates on Earth. Young men and women, obviously clerks, stenographers, secretaries and other non-entities, scurried about intent on the activities that set clerks, stenographers and secretaries a-scurrying. An occasional junior executive type would pass, less hurriedly. Senior executives evidently kept to their offices, or possibly had already called it a day by this hour; senior executives can afford to be more philosophical about the time length of their labors and seldom indeed work a swing or graveyard shift.

He was directed to elevator twenty which was evidently expecting him. The screen gave him no reply when he said, "Miss Sophia Anastasis' apartment." The door closed and they rose for what seemed to him an extraordinary long time.

When it stopped, a voice said, "Put your identity card in the slot, please."

He muttered, "At this rate, it'll be worn out in no time." But he complied and the door opened.

He stepped out into a corridor which had no business building characteristics whatsoever. This floor, at least, was obviously devoted to living quarters.

A uniformed young efficient who could have been the twin of Antony Berch, the so-called Protective officer in Satellite City, or of Al Rich, up to and including the cold eyes, was there. Rex Bader wondered inwardly and sourly whether it was an in-born characteristic of the people connected with the Syndicate. Did they all have cold, empty eyes?

The other said, "Mr. Bader? May I see your identity card, please?"

He brought it forth, handed it over for the other's inspection.

"Thank you, sir. You are expected. Miss Anastasis' is the Green Suite. That way, sir."

They didn't even number or letter them. The Green Suite, yet.

It was identified by a square jade set into the door. There was no recognizable identity screen. Rex Bader shrugged and looked for a bell, or some other means of bringing attention to himself. Possibly he should knock.

It seemed awfully plebian, in this ultra-swank atmosphere.

The door opened and she was there.

He had met her before, some time ago on an earlier job, and now it came back to him, how truly beautiful a woman she was. Save for Gina Angel, he couldn't remember ever having seen a brunette of such poised pulchritude. She was taller than Gina and at least a decade older, but her complexion, her hair, her nature-red lips and her aristocratic nose were so basically similar that he wondered if they were related. It could well be. Possibly all these Syndicate people he was coming into contact with were related, distantly or otherwise.

She was dressed in a simple cocktail-time outfit. Simple, but so obviously the product of one of the most expensive peddlers of *haut couter* of Copenhagen, Rio, or perhaps Budapest. She put out a hand, in the man-like fashion he remembered.

"Mr. Bader. How good of you to come." She had a glass of champagne in her other hand.

He shook and said, smiling ruefully, "An invitation from Miss Sophia Anastasis is a command." He paused and added, "Otherwise, she might send around a couple of the boys to bring you."

She laughed gently. "Oh, come now, Mr. Bader. We're not as uncivilized as all that." She turned and led the way back to the living room.

He was mildly surprised at the fact that they were evidently alone and also that the Green Suite was comparatively small. Not by the standards of his mini-apartment, of course, but certainly it wasn't the multi-servant staffed apartment he had expected of Sophia Anastasis. He wasn't quite sure of the position she held but he knew very well that it was high in the councils of International

Diversified Industries, Incorporated which was, for all he knew, as gigantic an operation as the Satellite City Authority in the workings of the Syndicate.

She motioned him to a comfort chair near the window, a window that oversaw Manhattan spectacularly. They must have been very near to the top of the skyscraper.

Without asking his preference, she brought him a glass of champagne from the tiny bar at one end of the room. And she must have caught his surprise at the somewhat modest quality of her quarters.

She said, "Now what did you expect, Mr. Bader? Ostentation and bad taste?"

He shrugged and tasted the vintage wine. "Certainly not, but possibly a servant or two—at least."

She put her own glass down on a cocktail table, after choosing a chair across from him.

She said, "You finally get to the point where you hate servants, and take every opportunity to escape from them. Among other places, I have a chalet in Austria with a staff of at least twenty. I seldom am in residence. Did you ever hear that pathetic story about Queen Elizabeth and Prince Philip?" Without waiting for an answer, she said, "They had a very small apartment in the bowels of Buckingham Palace. Very middle-class. It had a kitchen, a bathroom, a small living room, dining room, complete with record player and TV set. They would invite only their very closest friends to this retreat. Elizabeth would cook, Philip would open the beer. They'd sit around and watch TV, or tell stories, or play Scrabble or Canasta. That sort of thing."

Rex Bader tastes his wine and said, "What did you wish to see me about, Miss Anastasis?"

"I have a message for you," she said, taking up her own glass again.

"Oh? Who from?"

"Uncle Nick. He said to tell you that your twenty-five thousand pseudo-dollars is deposited to your account in the Satellite City Bank. Evidently, Uncle Nick rather likes you, Mr. Bader."

"No, he doesn't. Big Nick Mangano doesn't like anybody, except maybe Gina Angel and that's possibly a very old man's mistake. You don't survive five or six generations in the Mafia by allowing yourself to like anybody."

"Mafia is a rather silly word, these days, Mr. Bader. At any rate, Uncle Nick informed us that if anything happened to you, he would be terribly upset."

Rex grunted. "I'll just bet he worded it that way. He wants to maintain the image. If anything happened to me, he's afraid the Inter-American Bureau of Investigation would assume he was responsible and he doesn't want any black marks on the Satellite City record. But you didn't have to call me all the way over here and waste a glass of champagne to boot, just to deliver that message, Miss Anastasis. What else?"

She got up and went over to the bar and brought the magnum of champagne from its ice bucket and returned to fill their glasses. She put the bottle down on the cocktail table between them and reseated herself.

She said, "How is business, Mr. Bader?"

He looked at her. "Not too good. Right at present I'm unemployed."

"Oh? But the Satellite City assignment must have paid rather well."

"Not too badly. But I'm a bachelor. They'll tax most of it away. However, for a while I'll be off Negative Income Tax."

"Diversified pays in cash for special types of employment. Or, for that matter, it could be deposited to your account in Satellite City, the way Uncle Nick deposited your twenty-five thousand. The bank there is very . . . discreet, Mr. Bader."

"You are obviously offering me a job. What?"

She said easily, "You just mentioned that you were unemployed which means that the government assignment is now over. This *job* would involve very little in the way of effort and you would be recompensed very well."

"What is it?"

"This morning you reported to the Octagon. We have many resources, Mr. Bader, but it is difficult to crack the security that applies to the inner offices of Mr. Harrigan. I doubt if even many of the very highest officials in the government were aware of the meeting that took place there this morning and the surprising people who attended it."

"I wouldn't know," he said. "They weren't introduced to me." He came to his feet.

She said, "What was Colonel Simonov doing there?"

He shook his head. "In my business, if you shoot off your mouth about the business of the people who have hired you, you don't last long. I'd hate to get the reputation, even with you people, of being a blabbermouth. Frankly, I'm afraid of such folk as your Al Rich. They can get obnoxious, especially when they have available such characters as Rocky to handle the rough stuff."

She took another sip of her champagne and ignored the fact that he obviously was ready to leave.

"Cousin Al can be a bit . . . impetuous. Is that where you acquired your discolored eye?"

"Yes, and a few discolored ribs and odds and ends to go along with it. I'm afraid I'll have to be leaving, Miss Anastasis. Tell Big Nick thanks, but I'm afraid that if I accepted the twenty-five gran' the revenue people would just tax me out of it anyway. That would put me in the ninety percent bracket."

She said impatiently, "Don't be a fool. There is no record of that anywhere except Satellite City. You can draw on it any time you wish. Not in this country, of course. Then there would be a record. But almost anywhere else in the world."

"And have an income tax evasion rap hanging over my head, if and when it was discovered? No thanks. Big Nick himself was sent over for tax evasion and I don't have the pull he had to get out of it."

"That's up to you, of course. The amount will remain on deposit, in case you think it over. Meanwhile, what were Colonel Simonov and Ambassador Wilkonson and Georg Bonnet doing at that meeting this morning? What else did they want of you, beyond your report on Satellite City?"

"I've never even heard of Georg Bonnet," he told her. "I didn't lie to you. I don't want any trouble with you people. I'm smart enough for that. But I also can't discuss the business of a client. If I ever *did* do any work for Diversified you'd want the same discretion. If I betrayed them, how do you know I wouldn't do it to you?"

She was miffed, but it wasn't Sophia Anastasis' style to show anger. She stood and saw him to the door.

There, she said, "You have a priority on my personal phone in case you change your mind, Mr. Bader."

"Thanks."

XIV

He returned to New Princeton and to his mini-apartment and thought about it.

He sat in the sole comfort chair his mini-apartment boasted and took it up piece by piece, those pieces he had at his disposal, and tried to weave them together.

He ordered himself a simple dinner at his autotable and scowled at it. While he had been there at Sophia Anastasis' alleged modest suite, why hadn't he dropped a hint that he could use a sandwich? She probably would have ordered up a few pounds of caviar, a half-ton of smoked salmon, and a side of real corned beef. Damn it, why couldn't he remember to free-load when he had the chance? That champagne she had served him probably cost her something like a hundred pseudo-dollars. Not that she would have known, or cared.

A quarter of a million Common Europe mark-francs, and tax free.

The devil with the dinner. Not only did he not eat the napkin and plate, he discarded most of the whale hash and the hydroponics grown brussel sprouts, and simply sneered at the soy bean ice cream.

That period of acting the multi-millionaire had spoiled him spitless.

A quarter of a million pseudo-dollars. Ché Djilas must really be a razzle. He wondered what motivated the man. Which brought to mind the fact that somehow Ché

Djilas was able to swing the finances that allowed him to go to ground in Satellite City. The theory was that radicals were usually on the threadbare side, living in garrets and eating black bread and cabbage and so forth. In Satellite City you ate black bread only if you liked it and with Danish *sil* and sour cream, or whatever, to go along with it.

Where in the hell did a wild-haired weird like Ché Djilas ever get the funds to make Satellite City his hideout?

And then a germ of an idea began to grow. Perhaps he knew the answer to that one.

He spent the next three days largely at the TV library booster screen. He read, or at least skimmed, everything he could find in the National Data Banks on the Black Hand, the Mafia, the Camorra, the Cosa Nostra, The Syndicate. He was surprised how little there was, particularly anything recent. He suspected it was no accident. Publicity was a two way street, as Scoop Ericsson had pointed out. You could either buy it, or, with the same money, suppress it.

At midnight of the third day, he took his pocket identity phone-card out and placed it on the desk. He left the mini-apartment and went to the elevator bank, but then hesitated and shook his head. He went to the stairs and descended two more floors to the tenth basement level of the high-rise apartment building, avoiding even the minor matter of his ordering an elevator to transport him being recorded in the data banks.

He made his way to *Jerry's Joynt*, his favorite autobar-club and the nearest thing he had to a hangout. He wasn't much of a hand at hanging out in bars, even if he could have afforded it, especially when he was on Negative Income Tax.

Inside, he found the place sparcely occupied. Those present were largely seated before the ultra-large Tri-Di screen which dominated one end of the clubroom. Rex Bader finally located one whom he knew reasonably well and approached his table. The other's eyes were glued to the show, an ultra-violent war thing, and more than realistic.

Rex bent over him and said, "Hey, Charlie, I forgot my pocket phone. Left it in the apartment. Could I borrow yours? I want to make a call."

Theoretically, it was illegal to allow your pocket phone, identity card out of your own possession. But that was theory. Charlie, invariably on Negative Income Tax, had nothing to lose. Without taking his eyes from the slaughter on the screen, he handed it over. He knew very well that Bader couldn't use it to order a drink, an identifying thumbprint was necessary for that or any other purchase.

Rex Bader took the phone down to a table, remote from anyone else, and flicked back the cover. He activated the phone, but not the screen, and said into it, "Information," and then, "The private residence of John Mickoff, assistant to Howard Harrigan of the Inter-American Bureau of Investigation."

John Mickoff faded in, scowling sleepily. He had obviously been awakened and was obviously in bed and speaking into a phone screen sitting on a night table.

He muttered, "What in the hell do you want? Who is this?"

Bader could see him, but the government agent's own screen would be blank.

Rex said, "Can you scramble this?"

The other was mystified. "Yes. Why?"

"Do it."

"All right, it's done."

Bader activated the screen on his borrowed phone so that his image could now be seen.

"Bader," Mickoff grumbled. "What the hell do you want this time of night?"

"Are you sure this call is scrambled? No record of it anywhere? No possible way anybody could be bugging this conversation?"

"If there is, it's something our department doesn't know about. What in the devil do you want?"

"I want to talk to you. Personally. Anything that can be scrambled can be unscrambled."

John Mickoff rolled his eyes upward. "Come to the office in the morning, chum-pal."

"No. I don't want to come to the office. I want to see you personally, somewhere where there's no chance of there being a bug."

Mickoff stared at him, finally having come full awake. "All right, Bader. Come here. The address is Apartment 1009, Tenth Floor, Midas Building, Lincolnville, Greater Washington. I don't leave here until eight-thirty in the morning."

"Coming."

It was pushing four o'clock by the time that he presented himself at Apartment 1009. He had taken the public transportation only to within a mile of Mickoff's high-rise apartment building in Lincolnville and had walked the rest of the way. He had avoided taking the elevator and climbed the ten floors. Now, at the door, he held a handkerchief over his face, in front of the identity screen.

John Mickoff opened up, finally. He was in pajama bottoms, but not tops. Rex Bader followed him in.

Mickoff, obviously once again roused out of sleep, growled, "Younger brother, what in the hell's going on?"

Rex Bader returned the handkerchief to his pocket.

He said, "Quick. I just walked up the stairs from the street. Do the building computers have any record of it?"

"Of course. You might as well have taken the elevator. There's an eye on every floor."

"Can you wipe it off the record? If you can, do it soonest. I don't want there to be any record of this visit, anywhere."

"Hold it a minute," Mickoff said. He led the way into the living room.

The apartment was approximately three times the size of that of Rex Bader and well done. Obviously a fellow bachelor, John Mickoff had also obviously put years into making his quarters a home. The place was *lived in*. Furnished man-style, warm, comfort predominating over all else; there wasn't a status symbol in sight. Rex Bader sighed. There were pictures, real books, photographs, even a gun rack.

Mickoff sat down at his desk and spoke urgently into his phone screen. After a moment, his voice took on a cold, official tone.

Meanwhile, Rex had brought a seeming auto-stylo from an inner pocket and was carrying it around the room, presenting it to pictures, to furniture, to the Tri-Di set, the phone screen, even the autobar.

John Mickoff took time off to stare at him. "What in the hell do you think you're doing, younger brother?"

"Mop," Bader said brieuy. "Is there any chance at all that this apartment is bugged?"

Mickoff rolled his eyes upward in despair, said, "For

144

crissakes," and returned to his phone screen without bothering to answer.

Finally, he got up and headed for his dining alcove. He said over his shoulder. "Right. There's no record of you entering this building, and when you leave, chumpal, there'll be no record of that, either. Coffee?"

"Yes."

John Mickoff returned shortly with a whole pot of coffee and two cups. "Black?"

"Yes."

Scratching the black wiry hair on his chest, sleepily, the assistant to Howard Harrigan poured. Rex Bader had sunk into one of the old style leather easy chairs. Where had Mickoff found these wonderful museum pieces?

John Mickoff said, "What's it all about?"

Rex Bader said carefully, "That group at the Octagon the other morning. How many of them could be gotten to by Diversified Industries, or the Satellite City Authority?"

Mickoff stopped pouring. "Are your eggs completely scrambled?"

"Lucky Luciano was pardoned by a governor of New York, back in the old days. Big Nick Mangano had to go higher than that. His pardon came through the Federal government."

"I see what you mean," Mickoff said, finishing the filling of their cups. He handed one to Bader, took a seat himself.

He said, finally, "That's not the way it works, you know. Somebody doesn't just come up to the governor with a hundred thousand pseudo-dollars, or whatever, and say, 'Here. Pardon Lucky.'"

"What does he say?"

"Politics are ever the same. It's a matter of you scratch

my back and I'll scratch yours and over and over again. You don't get anywhere in politics without compromises, without doing favors to get favors. To get elected, even men of the caliber of Roosevelt had to depend on corrupt city machines such as Frank Hague's in New Jersey, Kelly-Nash in Chicago, Pendergast in Kansas. Roosevelt was nominated, the first time, by Huey Long. To get the support of those people, he had to give in return. The same thing applied to your governor.

"Let's make it up as we go along. The arms of various politicians in New York City, say, were twisted. They got on the phone and said to the next man, higher up, 'Listen, if you want to swing the Italian vote in this Borough, next election, you'd better see what you can do to get Charlie Luciano pardoned.' Other calls were being made, to other politicians. One gets an offer of fifty thousand dollars for his next campaign fund—if Luciano is pardoned. Another gets a threat that if Luciano isn't pardoned certain facts will come out that he isn't interested in having revealed."

"I get the message," Rex Bader said.

Mickoff nodded. "After awhile, the governor has too much pressure being brought on him to be able to ignore. He's a practical politician. He needs the support of these people who are clamouring for Lucky's pardon. He finds some kind of excuse, or other, and complies. Probably hating himself as he does it."

Bader nodded. "Okay. Great. How many of those present the other morning could be gotten to?"

John Mickoff thought about it, unhappily. "The Common Europe and the Americans, yes. Given time. It would take time. I don't think you could get to Simonov. They've got a different set-up. But I could be wrong." He

146

thought some more. "I don't believe that anybody could put pressure to bear on Ambassador Wilkonson. He's the old style Britisher. The king himself couldn't order him to betray what he considered his code of honor."

"How about the Americans? How about Harrigan, your boss?"

Mickoff took a deep regretful breath. "Mr. Harrigan receives his orders directly from the White House or the Attorney General. And when he gets them, he takes them."

"And, as you pointed out, it was Huey Long who nominated F.D. Roosevelt the first time. And you might have added that the Mafia affiliated Pendergast machine sponsored his last vice-president."

Mickoff looked at him bleakly. "What are you driving at, younger brother?"

"Can they get to you?"

"That's what I thought you were coming to. I take my orders from Mr. Harrigan." ·

"Who, when he gets orders from higher up, takes them."

John Mickoff's hand was shaking as he poured them more coffee. "One thing you might want to know about, Bader. I never knew my father, except very vaguely as a child. I remember him as the most gentle, the kindliest and the . . . the most beautiful man who ever lived. He was shot to death, by accident, in possibly the last jurisdictional gang war between the Brooklyn families of the Cosa Nostra. He was coming home from work, an innocent bystander, as the expression goes. Probably the greatest motivating factor in my becoming a glorified cop when I grew up."

"Okay. Great. But you still take your orders."

"Yep. At least, so far I have. Maybe there'll come a time when I can't. If I don't, I'll soon be making my living collecting Negative Income Tax."

"Okay. We get to the big question. Suppose that nobody knew what you were doing? That is, nobody higher up, or lower down, or anywhere else, who could start pulling strings?"

John Mickoff came to his feet and went over to his autobar. In a few moments he came back with two shot glasses.

"Rum,' he said, and poured them into the coffee cups. He added more of the hot black coffee. "All right. You want to take a crack at that quarter of a million pseudo-dollars."

Rex Bader said carefully, "That's part of my motivation. I also owe a bust in the nose to a character up in Satellite City."

XV

John Mickoff looked at him long and thoughtfully. "If you were thinking of taking on the assignment, why were you so emphatic about rejecting it the other morning?"

Rex Bader was disgusted. "Possibly because I didn't see an opening I see now. Possibly because of what we've been talking about this past fifteen minutes. Several of those at the meeting can be approached by Diversified Industries or the Satellity City Authority, particularly given time. Sophia Anastasis already smells a rat, she's tried to bribe me."

"Why me? As I've already pointed out, I take orders."

"I've got to trust somebody. I need quite a bit of help. For instance, wasn't it you who arranged that queer unlimited number account at the Grundbank for me in the name Harold Brown?"

"Yes. I handled the whole thing, we wanted to keep the information as restricted as possible. We made it unlimited since we didn't know just how much you'd need. It was backed by Mr. Harrigan's secret emergency fund."

"Okay. There's one thing I forgot to report when I told Harrigan and you about that final scene with Al Rich and Rocky, possibly because at the time my brains were slightly scrambled. At any rate, Rich told me the hundred thousand pseudo-dollars would be transferred back to my account in the Grunsbank."

John Mickoff did a silent whistle. "So?"

"So when you cancel the account, don't bother to mention the details to Harrigan, but leave the hundred thousand there. We'll need a war chest."

"Huuum. And what else?"

"You've got a big staff to order around. I want the complete plans of the Satellite City orbital hotel."

"That oughten to be too difficult. They do their assembling and welding and so forth up there but practically all the engineering, interior decorating and so forth must be done on Earth. The plans will be somewhere in the data banks, or otherwise available. What else?"

"I want papers that will at least temporarily give me a little weight to throw around. Make me a special agent of the Inter-American Bureau of Investigation, or something. Can you do that without Harrigan finding out?"

Mickoff thought about it, sipping away at his coffee. "I should be able to. He doesn't bother with details. And any orders I give are assumed to have his approval. I'm his right hand and part of his left, for that matter. He could kick off tomorrow and it'd be months before anyone noticed. What else?"

"I can't think of anything else, right now.

"How do you figure on getting into Satellite City without spilling the beans, or at least without arousing their suspicions? They're not stupid, you know."

"Secret," Rex Bader said, standing. "When can I have the agent's identification?"

"I'll arrange it tomorrow. I won't even have to see you. It'll go through on your present identity card." Then Mickoff said, casually, "What happens to the reward, assuming you ever get this Ché Djilas?"

"We split it three ways, and retire."

"I'll probably have to retire. Even if we pull it off the old man will bounce me when he finds out I've done all this behind his back. I must be crazy. Why three?"

"I need another man to work with me in Satellite City. If I can't locate the one I need, the whole project is off. By the way, how do I know Djilas when I arrest him? If nobody's seen him . . ."

"None of our people have seen or photographed him, but we have various witnesses in those two countries where he managed to overthrow the ruling regimes who hate his guts. Bring him down, alive, and they'll identify him. Or if you have to shoot him, get a photo of his face . . . dead."

"Okay." Rex Bader turned to head for the door and the other followed him.

"One thing, younger brother."

"Yeah?"

"Don't underestimate this Ché Djilas. He's probably the most dangerous man in the world. There are a lot of people no longer around because of Ché and if he ever gets really underway in some country like India or Indonesia there's going to be a great many more. They take their revolutions seriously in South Asia."

Professor Christopher Moselle kept him waiting approximately fifteen minutes in the anteroom of the professor's offices in the high-rise administration building of Southern University City. The other wasn't being coy. There was a continual stream of students, secretaries and what Rex Bader assumed were assistants of one type or the other. The professor's department was obviously a sizeable one.

Eventually, a little blonde wearing a minus-skirt, and

the yellowist shirt Bader could off-hand ever remember seeing, came trotting in and told him the professor could spend a short time with him.

The professor's *sanctum sanctorium* was ultra-modern but the professor wasn't. He sported an antique Van Dyke beard and a bedraggled suit that must have been at least three decades out of style. Right now he looked harassed.

"Sorry,'" he said to Rex Bader, half rising to shake hands. "Beginning of the new term. Chaos."

"Thanks for seeing me at all," Bader said. "I understand that you're the head of the Parapsychology Department. You must be busy." He found a chair before the other's desk and sat down and projected an air of great earnestness. "Nevertheless, this is a matter of national importance, Professor Moselle."

The other blinked at him. "I can't imagine. Forgive me. Your identification, Mr. uh, Bader?"

Rex Bader brought his pocket phone and handed it over the desk. "I work directly under John Mickoff, first assistant to Howard Harrigan of the Inter-American Bureau of Investigation."

The professor said things into one of his phone screens, then put Bader's credentials into the slot. He waited a moment, then said, "Mr. Mickoff, I have a man here who calls himself Rex Bader." He listened a moment, then said, "Yes, of course. Ordinarily, your bureau would seem to be somewhat out of my field. However, any cooperation I can give, of course."

He flicked the phone off and turned back to Rex, obviously still astonished. He handed back the other's pocket phone.

"Sir," Rex said, "this is of such vital importance that I

must have your pledge that anything I say to you will never be repeated. Not even to your wife, Professor."

"Very well, sir. You have that pledge. Now what can I possibly do for you?"

"I have read up, in the past couple of days, a bit on parapsychology, or do you prefer to call it extrasensory perception?"

The professor shrugged. "Or psionics, for that matter."

"We are particularly interested in psychokinesis. I understand that there are some other terms."

"Telekinetic abilities, parakinesis, or PK. Our field, like any other science has gobblydygook terminology. In layman terms, the power of mind over matter."

"Science?" Rex Bader said evenly.

"Yes, science."

Rex cleared his throat. "Before we go any further could you tell me a little more about the human mind being able to move physical objects?"

"I thought you said you had read up a bit on the field."

"I did. Frankly, I am sceptical."

"You shouldn't be. Parapsychology, along with other sciences, has been enjoying some remarkable breakthroughs in the past few decades. However, it has been with us down through the ages. Not only parakinesis, but telepathy, clairvoyance, precognition, clairaudience . . ."

"That last one is new to me."

"The ability to hear over distances, or other obstacles, beyond the ordinary."

"Okay. But my particular interest is parakinesis."

"Very well. Have you ever heard of Eusapia Palladino?" At the other's shake of head, Professor Moselle went on. "I use the example since it is so well authenticated. I too have my doubts about most of the mediums and would-be magicians who perform for the public. However, Miss Palladino was a phenomenon who appeared circa 1900. She was an ignorant, uneducated nymphomaniac Italian peasant girl who hadn't the vaguest idea of how she accomplished the things she did. Nevertheless, she did them before literally scores of the most eminent scientists of the time and she did them many times under laboratory conditions for such notables as both of the Curies, Oliver Lodge, Courtier, Favre, Ochorowicz, oh, I could name a good many more, top men and women in all the sciences. She did not perform in darkened rooms, which she had had opportunity to, ah, gimmick up, beforehand, Mr. Bader."

"What did she do."

"She lifted, without touching, such objects as heavy tables that she could not have lifted physically even if she had touched them. She levitated over and over again, sometimes taking her chair with her, to go drifting about the room at ten feet or more above floor level."

"I see. And there have been other examples?"

"Down through the ages. In the past, the superstitious thought in terms of witches, devils, warlocks and so forth. We will never know how many unfortunates were rewarded with a stake through their hearts or being burned alive because they exercised out of the ordinary abilities. Today, happily, we have taken the subject into the laboratory. I assure you, Mr. Bader, psionics are a reality. We are still in the infancy of exploring the science, but it is a science, not carnival fakery."

Rex Bader took a deep breath. "Great. I want to meet somebody who can exercise psychokinesis, somebody who has this telekinetic power."

"Why?"

"I can't answer that, Professor. It's top secret. However, I can tell you that such American officials as my superior, Mr. Harrigan, think it of utmost national importance."

"I see." The professor thought about it for a long moment. Finally he said, "As a coincidence, we have in this university city, at this time, a student who has exhibited a greater degree of telekinetic ability than any other I have tested in the past twenty years. My own particular field, currently at least, tends more toward precognition, but we explore all ESP phenomenon, of course."

"Could I meet him?"

The professor looked at his wrist chronometer, hesitated and muttered, "It's a bit early for lunch." But then he flicked on one of his desk phones and said, "Miss Andrews, will you please get in touch with Seymour Rice? I believe he is a junior, this year. Request that he have lunch with me at the faculty auto-cafeteria. My usual table."

The screen said something and the professor turned back to Rex Bader. "Obviously, I am somewhat intrigued. I am not usually the cocktail in the middle of the day type, but would you like to join me, before lunch? I'm sure that young Rice will not be there for another twenty or thirty minutes."

Seymour Rice proved a disappointment at first sight, at least. He was a tallish, gangling kid who looked no more than nineteen or twenty, although that would seem unlikely if he was already a junior. He had unkempt red hair, freckles, a much too prominent Adam's apple, and was gawky and uncomfortable in the presence of professors and strangers older than himself. Whether or not he shaped up better in the company of contemporaries, Rex

Bader wouldn't know, but he had a suspicion that the other had some years to go before he achieved ease in intercourse with his fellows.

The professor introduced them, failing, as pre-instructed, to mention Rex Bader's connections with the Bureau.

They sat at the professor's table which was at a reasonable distance from any other, and ordered.

The professor looked at the menu of the day, set in the table top and said dismally, "Do you think food will ever come back?"

Rex Bader said, "No. When you finally get to the point where plates, napkins and utensils are all edible, rather than having to be washed, you've passed the point of no return."

He spent the period of eating sizing the young man up. He had hoped for someone a bit more sophisticated, less an adolescent. What was taking place with the world's youth? A century before a man was considered a young adult at the age of fifteen or so. He took his place on the farm, or in the mine or mill, and was a man among men. Now, with present school requirements, you weren't a part of the adult world until in your mid-twenties. He didn't wonder at the frustration found among the college kids in this age. You became sexually aware and had your physical growth in your mid-teens, but you remained, in the eyes of society, an adolescent for the next decade.

When they had disposed of the remnants of their meal in the center of the table, and the scraps had descended into the bowels of the restaurant, Rex Bader said to young Rice, "The professor tells me that you are his expert on psychokinesis."

The others Adam's apple bobbed. "Well . . . well, yes sir. That is, I helped the professor in some of his ESP experiments. I don't know much about it, but it's very interesting."

"How do you do it?"

Seymour Rice looked at him blankly.

The professor put in, "That is one of our problems, Mr. Bader. We still don't know. The ability is dormant, or possibly non-existent in the majority. Some have it to the tiniest degree. Some, like Mr. Rice, here, have a surprising quantity. If we could isolate the source of the ability, perhaps we could intensify it, or bring it out in all." He smiled wanly. "And then the question would become, is it desirable that the race be able to exercise telekinetic powers? Happily, that is out of my field and others will have to answer."

Rex Bader brought a small ivory ball from his pocket and put it in the center of the table.

"A roulette ball," he said. "Let me see you move it."

Seymour Rice frowned and looked at Professor Moselle in question.

The professor nodded encouragement. "Pray try to demonstrate, Seymour."

The youngster ran a hand through his flaming hair, mussing it still further, bobbed his Adam's apple twice and stuck the tip of his tongue out the side of his mouth, at which Rex Bader inwardly groaned.

Seymour Rice stared at the ivory ball. He looked up and said, "Could I bring it a little closer?"

Rex Bader said, taken aback at the request, "Okay. Let me see you move it."

The boy brought the roulette ball to within about two feet of his face and stared at it again in rapt concentration. The day was, if anything, a bit coolish but there were blisters of sweat on his forehead.

The ball stirred and rolled possibly one inch.

XVI

Seymour Rice slumped back into his chair, brought forth a handkerchief and wiped away the perspiration.

Rex looked at the professor. "You mean, that's all?"

"My dear Mr. Bader, so far as science is concerned, parakinesis has been proven. He could have moved a mountain and it wouldn't have been proven more definitely."

"But earlier you mentioned this Italian peasant girl who could float tables all around the room."

"See here. What is it that you really want, Mr. Bader?"

"I want somebody who can do more than budge that perfectly round ivory ball an inch or so."

"I see." The professor stood. "Come along to the laboratory. You said you had looked a bit into parapsychology. Evidently, you didn't look very far. Seymour, is it possible for you to devote the balance of the afternoon?"

"I . . . I suppose so, Professor."

Still unhappy, Rex Bader followed them, not having the vaguest idea of what was up. He pocketed his ivory ball.

Professor Moselle wordlessly led them to the elevators and they dropped to the basement level which housed the building's metro station. There he summoned a four-seater vehicle and gave the direction for their destination.

They emerged into another building's metro station which contained a considerably larger percentage of scurrying students than had the administration building. The professor led the way to what were evidently faculty elevators, and hence not so jam-packed, and they ascended a dozen or more floors.

When they emerged into the sterile hall of a university building devoted to classrooms and laboratories the professor muttered, "There will be no one here. The Parapsychology classes have yet to begin."

Rex Bader shrugged to himself. It was their top, they could start spinning it how and when they would.

The laboratory, if that is what it could be called, was sizeable and littered with equipment most of which Rex Bader couldn't have begun to identify with the exception of a standard size pool table and a card shuffler of the type used in casino's blackjack set-ups.

The professor said to Bader and Seymour Rice, "Wait here a moment," and left the room.

Just to be saying something, Rex said to Seymour Rice, "How did you find out you had this . . . ability?"

The younger man shuffled his feet. "Well, uh, the way it is, at the beginning of each new term, Professor Moselle requests that all freshmen take some basic tests. They don't *have* to, of course, but most do. It's kind of interesting. They've got a lot of IBM machines to sort it all out. And then, if your card is selected, then the professor and his staff request that you take some more tests that go a little further into it. Finally, they get down to the point where they have perhaps a hundred or so freshmen and then the professor gives them a little talk and requests that they all take Parapsychology One as one of their courses. And most of them do. It's really interesting. Kind of funny, but interesting."

The professor returned with a syrette. He said, "You're sure you don't mind, Seymour? This is your first booster, this term. You'll probably have a bit of reaction."

"No, sir, I don't mind." The student bared his arm and the professor injected him expertly.

Moselle said, "Now let us go over here and sit down for a time."

All three took student's desks and the professor said, "This will take a few minutes. Now, Mr. Bader, what has to be brought home to you is that we have made some breakthroughs in the field since the early days of investigation into ESP phenomenon and when such pioneers as Whately Carington and S.G. Soal in England and the Duke University people were working at guessing cards and pictures. At that time, fellowships were established at Cambridge and Harvard and a full scale laboratory was opened in the University of Utrecht. The Russians were also active in the University of Leningrad, but much of their research was kept confidential—as usual.

"Early in the experiments, Mr. Bader, they attempted to stimulate extrasensory perception with chemicals. Alcohol, for instance, which was soon discovered to be a depressent rather than a stimulant to ESP. They had a little success in some subjects with caffeine and nicotine, but to no great degree. It was with the coming of the hallucinogens, or, if you will, the psychedelics, that we began to get results. No, no, not with LSD or even mescaline, neither of which could be depended upon in spite of the claims made by the early non-professionals who experimented upon themselves—sometimes to their great sorrow. *Cannabis*, ah, marijuana, was also of little, if any, value, even when taken in the more pure form *charas* and eaten, rather than smoked. However, somewhat to the surprise of early investigators, it was found that the so-called sacred mushrooms of the Mexicans, *Psiolocybe mexicana,* which the Aztecs called, 'God's flesh,' actually did expand perception in many of our subjects. And contemporaries in Europe hit upon the fact that the *amanita muscaria* mushroom of Greece had much the same effect. Anthropologists, in my opinion, should go further into this. These were the mushrooms, by the way, eaten by the Centaurs, the horse-totem tribesmen of Ancient Greece; and were the so-called ambrosia of the gods."

The professor broke off and darted a look at his student.

"Ah," he said, "let us proceed." He stood and led the way over to the pool table. Seymour Rice came to his feet clumsily and followed, there was a strangeness in him.

The professor said to Rex Bader, "To make it brief, the first discovery in the expansion of metal perception as applied to ESP came with the isolation of psiolocybin in the laboratory. It was but the first step, but of great moment. And now . . ."

The three of them stopped at the pool table and the professor looked at Rex, a definite sly quality in the back of his eyes.

"The ball?"

Bader dug down into his pocket, scowling, came up with the ivory roulette ball and handed it over.

The professor tossed it to the center of the table. "Seymour!"

The ball began to move. It did a circle. It bounced up against one of the pool table sides. It did another couple of circles, and actually bounded two or three times, a few inches into the air.

Rex Bader, in utter disbelief, shot a quick look at the

younger man. Once again, there were blisters of sweat on the other's forehead, and his eyes were glaring like an early day horror movie actor playing Bram Stoker's *Dracula.*

Bader shot a look at Professor Moselle who was beaming at his protege. "How long can he keep that up?"

"Only for moments."

"What happens then?"

"It falls away entirely and it will be a week before he can take the drug again effectively."

"What drug?"

"Would you recognize the Latin if I told you? It is distantly related to psiolocybin—distantly."

"What happens to him now?"

"For a time he is in a slight daze. Then he becomes somewhat nauseated. Then he sleeps for possibly twelve hours."

Bader muttered unhappily. He said, "Could you let me have one of those syrettes?"

It was the professor's turn to be unhappy. "Good heavens, why?"

Bader looked at him. "I can't tell you. National security is involved."

The professor left the room, after making a hopeless gesture.

Rex Bader looked at Rice. The ball, on the table, had stopped moving. Rex said, "How're you feeling?"

The other giggled. "If you wore glasses, I could make them fall off and shatter."

"Oh, great. Could you break the arches of my feet?"

"I . . . I don't think so."

"Well, don't try it."

The professor came back, another of the syrettes in his hand. He was *very* unhappy. However, he handed it

162

over. "You realize, of course, that immediately after taking this and being subjected to it, he must be taken care of, supervised for a matter of hours. He is not lucid, after an hour or so."

"Is he lucid now?"

"Yes, of course. But he must be gotten home and into bed. The bad reaction starts in about an hour."

"I'll take him." Rex Bader looked into the eyes of Professor Moselle. "If you wish, check this out with John Mickoff, with whom you've already been in contact. Let me repeat, Professor, this is top-secret, top national security. From your accent, I deduce you were born in Common Europe."

"In Germany."

"Then I may add that we are cooperating with the top authorities of Common Europe. And, for that matter, if you have any off-beat ideological theories, with the officials of the Soviet Complex."

Seymour Rice muttered, "What goes on?"

Rex said, "Where does he live? I'll see him home. I have to talk with him."

"Then do it soon," the professor said. "In forty-five minutes to an hour, he will be useless to you."

"Where does he live?"

The professor told him.

Rex Bader led the younger man out of the laboratories to the elevators, and down to the metro station.

In the elevator, he said, "Have you ever stayed in a really first class hotel, and eaten in a three star restaurant?"

"Sure."

"You have, eh?"

"Sure," the other giggled.

"Have you ever worn evening clothes?" Rex Bader took in the, to him, unhappy student get-up.

"Ummm," the other giggled. "I sure have."

They reached the basement level of the metro and Rex Bader summoned a two-seater and instructed it as to their destination.

He said carefully, "Now, listen. How would you like to have a vacation in Satellite City? All expenses paid. And if everything goes well, you'll possibly wind up with something in the vicinity of a hundred thousand pseudo-dollars as a bonus, tax free. That's not guaranteed, but possibly."

"No thanks."

"What!"

"I've been to Satellite City and I don't like it. And I've got a hundred thousand dollars and a helluva lot more."

"Oh Lord, give me strength," Rex Bader said.

PART THREE

XVII

At first Rex Bader thought that Seymour Rice was already reacting to the psychedelic-related drug he had taken, but that wasn't it.

Bader said, "What do you mean, you've already been to Satellite City?"

Beyond being slightly high, which resulted in an occasional giggle, accompanied by a bobbing Adam's apple, Rice was seemingly still capable of carrying on an intelligent conversation.

He said, "My father took us all up to the orbiting resort hotel, four or five years ago. We spent a week. Some of it was very interesting, but free fall makes me sick. Father insisted that we experience the free fall gym and I became terribly nauseated."

"What do you mean, *all* of you?"

"The family. Mother, the three girls and my younger brother."

Bader closed his eyes in mute pain. "You mean your father can afford to take six people to Satellite City for a week?"

"Yes. Rice, Rice. I'm Seymour Rice the Third."

"I've never even heard of the first," Rex said bitterly. "You mean you're so loaded that you're not interested in making a quick, tax free hundred thousand pseudo-dollars?"

They had reached the building that was their destination, and the student, a bit wobbly mayhaps, led the way to the elevators.

On the way up, he said somewhat apologetically, "In spite of present taxes, Father has been able to find enough loopholes that all of we children will remain well-fixed. How *our* children will do, I couldn't say. They've got a tax on capital now."

"You mean a capital gains tax? They've had that for a long time."

"No. I mean a tax on capital. If you have a million dollars just sitting around, doing nothing, they tax it ten percent or so."

That was a new one to Rex Bader. He looked at the other. "At that rate, you'd be broke in ten years, no matter what you did."

"Or very nearly, although you can always spend it as fast as you can," the other said cheerfully, which was possibly the reaction to the drug, Bader decided wryly. Who could be cheerful about being done out of a million?

The apartment in which Seymour Rice the Third resided bore out his claims to affluence. These were not the quarters of an ordinary student making do on a shoestring.

The boy, evidently having gained some confidence as a result of the couple of hours spent with this stranger, glanced at his wrist chronometer and said, "Mr. Bader, I have a little more than half an hour. Then I'll have to be in bed. If you have anything you wanted to discuss with me. . . ." He let the sentence fade away, and gestured toward a chair.

Rex sat down and decided to give it a try.

"Look," he said. "I'm a special agent of the Inter-American Bureau of Investigation. You know, we inherited the term, G-Man. You can check that out with the professor, if you wish. Or, you can get in touch with my immediate superior in the Octagon."

"All right," you Rice said. Possibly being in his own territory, his own apartment, was giving him the new self possession.

Bader said, "Have you ever heard of Che Djilas?"

"Yes. Father says he is an unscrupulous scoundrel. When his followers took over in Trans-Africa, they nationalized the railroad without compensation. It was Father's railroad."

"Okay. Great," Rex Bader said. "That makes it a little easier. Ché Djilas probably has other revolts in mind. Has your father got any more railroads in the neutral countries?"

"I wouldn't know."

"The point is this. Ché Djilas has gone into hiding in Satellite City. They don't have any extradition laws there. In fact, they don't have any laws at all. However, it's gone beyond ordinary laws. Ché Djilas is evidently considered the most dangerous man in the world."

Seymour Rice was too young not to react to that. He shook his head, evidently in an attempt to ward off the increasing reaction to the drug and said, "What do you plan to do? Where do I come in?"

"I need your help in going to Satellite City and arresting him and bringing him back to Earth. Are you game?"

"Why . . . why, it sounds very interesting, but what could I do?"

"I can't tell you yet. I can't run the chance that you might, possibly inadvertently, blow the whole scheme."

"What do you want me to do?"

"In about a week I want you to go to Satellite City as an ordinary vacationist. Your cover is perfect, and pure luck. You've been there before. Your family is stinking rich, evidently. You can go without anybody thinking twice."

"Oh, mother and father would never approve of my leaving school, especially if I wasn't able to explain the whole thing to them. And father would never consent to my exposing myself to desperadoes such as Ché Djilas."

"How old are you?"

"Twenty-two."

"The hell with father."

Seymour Rice flickered eyes at that. You just didn't say that, evidently.

Rex Bader said, "I'll have fifty thousand pseudo-dollars transferred to your balance. Your people will never know anything about it. You won't be away from school for more than a week or two. You'll go to Satellite City and wait for me to show up. Go to the main gambling casino. I'll contact you there. Pretend not to know me when I first show up. Gamble every night, as though that was your main interest in visiting the place. Don't overdo it, but don't stint either. Take evening clothes. Play the part of the young rich man's son."

Seymour Rice the Third said, "I'm beginning to feel a little sick. I'd better get to bed."

Rex Bader looked at him. The kid's freckles did seem a bit faded.

Using the same ruse that he had the night before, that is, borrowing a pocket phone from an acquaintance in *Jerry's Joynt*, Rex Bader called John Mickoff again in his apartment. And once again he kept his screen deactivated.

When the other answered from his bed, Bader said, "This is you know who."

"Fine," the other growled. "Am I ever going to get any sleep in this razzle?"

"Do you know how to get in touch with Ilya Simonov?"

"Yes. Indirectly. It's a little complicated. Legally, of course, he's not supposed to be in this country. We tolerate him in much the same way they tolerate some of our people in Moscow."

"I want to talk to him."

"Why?"

"The less you know about the things I do, the better."

"All right. When?"

"The sooner, the better."

"All right. I'll let him know. He'll get in touch with you."

He spent the following morning at his library booster screen checking out everything he could find on Ché Djilas in the National Data Banks. For all practical purposes there was nothing. There were no photographs whatsoever and the three physical descriptions differed considerably, which set Bader back. Evidently, on several occasions during the chaos of the revolts the revolutionist had been instrumental in bringing off, he had granted interviews with newsmen. But on these occasions he had worn a mask. Obviously, he took every security measure he could.

It was a puzzling aspect. Rex Bader had vaguely been of the opinion that a revolutionist needed publicity almost as badly as did an entertainer. Would Hitler have ever been able to come to power if he had kept himself hidden and out of the public eye? Would Fidel Castro? You had to get out and spread your message, project yourself, influence your potential followers. Or, at least, so Rex Bader would have thought.

Of course, the moment you did reveal yourself to the public as a whole, you ran the chance of arrest or being shot down by your opposition. Possibly that was what motivated Ché Djilas. You can't arrest an unknown, which right now was one of Bader's big difficulties.

There was a knock on his door and he looked over at it. There was no face on the identity screen. Was the confounded thing out of repair? If it was, the computerized maintenance department of the building should have detected the fact and a repairman should have shortly turned up. He couldn't remember his identity screen being on the blink ever before.

He went over to the door and opened it. Colonel Ilya Simonov sauntered in. Before greeting him, Rex Bader scowled at the screen.

Simonov brought what looked something like an old fashioned fountain pen from his pocket. He said, laconically, "Scrambler. It blankets any electronic device within an area of about twenty feet, including bugs, when it's turned on."

Rex Bader said, "Come in, Colonel." He closed the door. Obviously, the other hadn't wanted a record of his visit.

The colonel looked about the tiny apartment. "Don't they do any better than this for you?"

"Do they do anything better than this for the average man over in the Soviet Complex?"

The colonel chuckled. "No. But you're not exactly an average man."

"I'm pretty damn average so far as income is concerned. If I'm working, as a single man I'm taxed so heavily that my income still remains only a fraction over the Negative Income Tax level. It's hard to beat."

The colonel said, "No wonder you've decided to take a

crack at that collection of rewards being offered for Ché Djilas." He lowered himself onto the couch which doubled as Rex Bader's bed during the sleeping hours.

Standing in the middle of the room, Rex Bader blurted, "How did you know that?"

Colonel Siminov said blandly, "I didn't until just the minute. However, it was a reasonable guess. Why otherwise would you want to see me again?" The first impression one received of the Soviet espionage head was one of easy goingness. However, the wolfish quality beneath the ease came through from time to time. Ilya Simonov was a lot of man.

Bader said, "Okay. Possibly I will. I'm looking into it."

"Why didn't you say so, there at the meeting?" the other said, curiously.

"Because the Syndicate is evidently backing Ché Djilas and the Syndicate has a lot of leverage. An informant of mine was of the opinion that of the ten persons present at that meeting only you and Ambassador Wilkonson couldn't be reached, in time."

"Why the Ambassador?"

"As the expression goes, he is a scholar and a gentleman—and very British."

The other laughed softly. "You are quite correct, so far as I am concerned. There is no Mafia, Cosa Nostra, Syndicate, or call it what you will, in the Soviet Complex. We have our own corruptions, perhaps, particularly among the politicians—what is there about politicians?—but we have no Mafia. Why did you want to see me?"

Rex Bader took the room's comfort chair and sat forward in it, elbows on knees, hands clasped. "Because I need all the help I can get and if you're uncorruptable by the enemy, you're one of the very few I can turn to.

"But one thing first. At the meeting the other morning, you said that the Soviet Complex does not want the revolts that Djilas is stirring up. This doesn't jibe with all the information emanating from your country since as far back as I can remember. Isn't the ultimate goal supposed to be world communism?"

The colonel was amused. "The ultimate goal, perhaps. But that can be rather ultimate. Right at this point further, ah, proletarian revolutions are impractical."

"I . . . I . . . don't . . . believe . . . you."

Ilya Simonov was patient. "My dear Bader, since its inception the present government of the area once known as Russia had been basically interested in the welfare of . . . Russia. Slogans, propaganda, high sounding, idealistic statements to the contrary, the interest has been in Russia. No one else actually counted. Some of our party theoreticians explained this by saying the long view made it necessary to protect the Soviet Union at all cost because ultimately it was the hope of the whole world. That it must be made strong, even at the cost of other peoples, so that *ultimately* it could bring the, ah, blessings of communism to the rest.

"Have you heard of the Spanish Civil War, Mr. Bader?"

"A little. When Franco came to power immediately before the Second World War."

"Yes. There was a revolutionary situation in Spain at that time. When Franco struck, large elements were in favor of forming a Soviet type government, taking over the industries and all else. However, Stalin was opposed to this. He was afraid that it would precipitate a war with Germany, Italy and other European countries that were afraid of Russia and communism. He couldn't afford a war. He was busy trying to industrialize. So the

Communist party in Spain, rather than advocate real revolution, took his orders, joined the United Front with the socialists, anarchists, and the Spanish equivalent of democrats and republicans, and proclaimed themselves nothing more than liberals. When the anarcho-syndicalists in Barcelona took matters into their own hands and began to seize the factories and so forth, Spanish communist divisions moved in on them and put them down.

"It's not the only example of Russian attempts to suppress revolution in other countries. When Tito seized power in Yugoslavia, Stalin tried to cool him down. He didn't want to antagonize the United States and Great Britain; he needed their help during the war. Following the war, Stalin tried to get Mao together with Chiang Kai-shek, once again afraid of stirring up the Western nations. Mao, of course, wasn't having any and went on with his attack, as Tito had earlier. There are other examples. When the Greek communists were fighting it out with the right wing elements there, the United States and England came to the assistance of their side, but Russia failed to help the Greek communists.

"No, Mr. Bader. The Russian government is opportunistic. It has been in the past, it is today. We *still* do not wish to upset our own applecart by disturbing the balance of power."

"Okay," Bader said. "For the present, I'll accept that. Something else. I've been checking all I can on this Ché Djilas. Practically nothing is known about him. He was interviewed a few times by the world press, but always in disguise. Do you people have anything on him that wouldn't be in our own data banks?"

Simonov said slowly, "If I were to hear his voice, I'd know him."

"You would?"

"Yes. You see, I was one of the newsmen who interviewed him once in Trans-Africa. My department, at the time, had a scheme to capture him, but it fell through. His security was excellent."

. "You have nothing else at all?"

"No. All information available to the Soviet Complex has been turned over to your people and your data banks."

"Just what is it he advocates? What is his program?"

"He advocates a Dictatorship of the Proletariat which at best is out of date in this age. At worst it is nonsense. When Lenin and the Old Bolsheviks took over in Russia in 1917, they proclaimed a Dictatorship of the Proletariat. Theoretically, the working class, which was in a minority at the time, was to dictate to the peasantry and to the remnants of the old society. In actuality, it was the Communist Party doing the dictating, a mere handful of persons, and they dictated *to* the proletariat as well as to everyone else. Whether or not this applied to the Russia of Lenin's time, it most certainly doesn't anywhere today."

Rex Bader muttered unhappily. He said finally, "I want to get in touch with Ambassador Wilkonson."

"That shouldn't be difficult, surely you know where the Common Europe Embassy is located."

Bader shook his head. "The Diversified Industries people, notably Miss Sophia Anastasis, think that I have withdrawn from government employment, as indeed I have. But they know and wonder about the Ambassador's presence at that meeting. If I was seen going to the Embassy, they would smell a rat. If I phoned him there, the phone would most likely be tapped. Would he come to a lunch with you?"

"Most likely. Once or twice in the past it has been necessary to have dealings with hm'.'

"Could you make a date with him at, say, some small restaurant you're reasonably sure isn't in any way connected with the Syndicate, and then let me show up instead?"

Simonòv said, "I know just the place. You can rest assured that there will be no bugs and no waiters in the secret employ of the estimable Miss Anastasis."

"How can you be so sure?"

"The colonel smiled wolfishly, even as he came to his feet. "Because they're all in my employ."

He looked down at Rex Bader. "There's just one thing I wish to make clear, Mr. Bader. In spite of what I have said, I am dedicated to my country. Time will solve, is solving, its current shortcomings and problems. To help her achieve that time, I am willing to give my life. I have proven that on various occasions."

Rex Bader also stood. He took in the tiny red ribbon in the other's lapel. The Hero's Combat Award.

"So I understand," he said.

XVIII

In the Octagon, as they walked along the corridor, Rex Bader said to Mickoff, "This fellow doesn't know anything about me?"

"Nothing at all."

"Don't introduce us. I don't want to know his name and I don't want him to know mine. By the way, what's the supposed reason for my coming here today?"

"To explain your expense account on the Satellite City job," John Mickoff grinned at him. "Younger brother, I've never seen such an expense account. That call girl in Tangier was the most highly priced mopsy in town."

"She wasn't a call girl. That was a nice girl. She just had expensive tastes. Besides, that was your instructions. I was a money heavy playboy looking for thrills."

"Did she give you any?"

"None of your business. By the way, you can cancel that special agent thing. I don't need it any more. Can you wipe all record of it from . . . from wherever it's recorded?"

"Yep, I can." John Mickoff tilted his head at him. "What did you need it for?"

"The less you know, the better."

"Younger brother, younger brother. I don't know why I'm sticking my neck out like this. Harrigan is going to have my fanny. On top of everything else, you have no more chance of pulling it off than I have of getting through the pearly gates."

They reached their destination and entered a long room which contained a long table covered with charts and blueprints and a single, jittery-looking individual who stood over them, clucking what seemed to be disapproval.

John Mickoff said, "Mr. Smith, meet Mr. Smith."

The other blinked owlishly from behind old-fashioned glasses. Rex Bader hadn't seen anyone in glasses, that he could remember, for years. When the other said, "Pleased to meet you," his instinct was to answer, "Why?" but he didn't. First glance told you that this one had no remotest sense of humor, no ability to dissimilate and was easy putty for anyone who wished to work him. Which was bad, and Rex Bader was going to have to do-something about it.

Rex shook hands very seriously.

He turned to the photostatic work on the table. "I'm interested in only a small part of the orbital hotel."

The other made a gesture at one of the large prints. "This is the hotel wheel." He squinted at Rex. "What is your interest?"

Mickoff said quickly, "That isn't of importance."

The other was miffed. "Very well. What do you wish to know?"

Rex Bader stared at the plans. "I'm no engineer. Where is the Galaxy Room?"

The other was scornful. He took a stylo from an inner pocket and pointed with it. "Here."

"And the gambling casino which adjoins it?"

"Right here."

Rex scowled unhappily. "Don't you have a larger blow-up?"

His informant went down to the other end of the table to a stack of papers that went about a yard square, and shuffled through them. He returned with one and spread it before Mickoff and Bader triumphantly.

It made a little more sense than had the larger blueprint.

Rex Bader pointed. "This is the Galaxy Room, and this the casino?"

"That is correct."

Rex pointed to the main entrance of the restaurant. "What kind of lock is on this door?"

The other stared down at the plans. "Why, why, I don't know."

"Can you find out?"

Mickoff said, "There must be some record, somewhere."

The expert said, perplexed, "I . . . I imagine. I can't imagine your interest."

Mickoff said, "That isn't of importance."

Rex Bader said, pointing, "And this is the door connecting the Galaxy Room and the gambling halls. What kind of lock is on it?"

"I have no idea. I don't even know if there is a lock."

Bader said thoughtfully, "There would be. Possibly not from the corridor into the restaurant, I don't know. But there'd undoubtedly be one to the casino."

Mickoff looked at him. "Important?"

"Very."

"We'll find out."

"Okay. Great. Let's go. Mr. Smith, a pleasure to meet you."

The other twitched and blinked. He said, "I don't know what this is all about."

Mickoff said, "You don't have to. Please remain here for a few minutes. I'll be back."

"Very well."

Rex Bader and John Mickoff went out into the corridor.

Rex said, "Can you put him in solitary for a week or so?"

"Oh, for *crissakes!*"

"Well, can you?"

"Why?"

"I don't want there to be the slightest chance that the Satellite City people learn that I was particularly interested in the layout of those rooms. If they got to that character he could no more keep his mouth shut than I could win the Olympic gold medal in marathon love making."

"They don't even know he's here."

"So you say. Can he get the information on the locks?"

"Probably, if there is any."

"I understand your bureau has some top security hideaways where you can keep people on the ice for indefinite periods. Stick him in such a place with a lot of first class grub and booze and a couple of girls—he looks as though he could use it."

Mickoff rolled his eyes upward.

"Well?"

"Yep, we can do it."

Rex Bader brought his pocketknife from his right trousers pocket. He handed it to the other.

"I've heard about your Department of Dirty Tricks, where you turn out all the fancy gismos. When you find out what kind of locks are on those doors, I want you to work up a gadget that will open them, whether they're electronic or whatever. Build the gadget into this knife, so that it looks as nearly the same as possible. The blades won't have to open. Just so it will pass slight scrutiny."

"Younger brother, you don't want much."

"Can you do it?"

"God only knows. I can turn the problem over to the boys. I've seen them bring out some doozies before. Look, do you want them to fix you up with some hideaway gun? You'll probably need it."

"No. I'd never get it through. They frisk you electronically when you first enter the hotel."

"These boys can build a laser gun into a belt buckle, or make one small enough to hide in the heel of your shoe."

"And thóse boys up there can detect it."

The restaurant was a small Italian one, the *Buca Lai*, and was in the way of being an anachronism since it sported all the attributes of days long past, from live waiters to red and white checkered table cloths and real linen napkins. You could still find them in Common Europe and in such cities as Tangier in North Africa, but they were mighty few and far between in the States.

When Rex entered, he spotted Ambassador Andrew Wilkonson at an isolated table in a corner. The Ambassador was looking at his wrist chronometer impatiently. He was a thin man and at least six and a half feet tall. He was about half bald and made no attempt to wear a wig, not to speak of having his own hair renewed by the new methods. Baldness was an affectation in this era.

Rex Bader approached and said, "Good afternoon, sir."

Wilkonson looked up, slightly irritated. "Oh, It's Mr. Bader, the investigator."

"Yes. Mind if I sit down?"

"Why, I have an appointment. Already overdue."

"I'm the appointment, Professor Wilkonson."

The other frowned. "What does that supposed to mean?"

"I had the Colonel arrange this meeting so that I could talk with you without either approaching the Embassy or phoning it."

"I see. Sit down, young man. A vermouth? Their Italian Martini and Rossi is jolly good here."

"Thanks, no," Rex said. He took the chair and came immediately to the point. "I've reconsidered that assignment Howard Harrigan and you others offered the other day."

"I see. Go on."

"If the attempt is to succeed as few persons as possible can be allowed to know that it is being made. I have not even so informed the Director of the Inter-American Bureau of Investigation. The way I see it, the principle foe is the Satellite City Authority, not Ché Djilas, and the Authority has informants and persons in positions of power who can bring pressure to bear just about everywhere."

Wilkonson nodded. "And why me?"

A waiter approached, but the ambassador waved him away.

Rex Bader said, "The clearer a picture I have of the whole thing, the better I'll be armed when I go up against Big Nick Mangano and his people. And some aspects of the picture aren't very clear."

"How can I help?"

Rex leaned forward slightly. "Representatives from the three great world powers were there at Harrigan's office. They branded this Ché Djilas the most dangerous man in the world, and were willing to pony up a quarter of a million tax free mark-francs, or its equivalent in other currency. But, in actuality, this mysterious Djilas, so far, has overthrown the governments of only two of the tiniest nations on Earth both of which have probably had a dozen or so other revolts, military and otherwise, in the past decade. Who gives a damn about whether or not Trans-Africa has a change in government? The whole thing doesn't ring true to me."

Wilkonson nodded. "Your point is well-taken. However, first, don't confuse superficial changes in the government, such as military revolt, with a basic revolution in which a socioeconomic system is altered. Ché Djilas is advocating basic changes, not just kicking out one president or dictator and installing another. Second, it is quite true that the countries in which he has been successful are tiny, but his prestige grows with each success. We are not worried about changes in such lands as Trans-Africa but if, say, India was to alter its politico-economic system world balance could well be thrown off."

Rex Bader thought about it. "Okay. But another thing. I'm no great student of political economy, or of the history of revolution, but I picked up along the line that revolutions are not caused by individual men, such as Ché Djilas, or even such as Fidel Castro, or Lenin and Trotsky, or, for that matter, Tom Paine, Sam Adams and Thomas Jefferson in this country. All these would have lived out their lives unnoticed if the conditions of their times had been different. Their countries were ripe for basic change, they were simply the leaders who stepped out in front, they were the sparks that lit the gunpowder barrel which was all set to go."

The ambassador nodded. "Go on."

"The point I'm trying to make, Professor, is that this Ché Djilas couldn't possibly do his subversive work in a prosperous, adjusted nation. He wouldn't get anywhere at all, here in the United States, for instance. Nor in Common Europe, nor, say, in Japan. He can only make way in backward, undeveloped countries where the people are restless and ready to listen to his message."

The ambassador's eyes narrowed slightly. "I am afraid that I misjudged your intelligence the other day, Mr. Bader. However, fundamentally you are correct. Continue to develop your point."

"The three most wealthy and powerful governments on Earth are being sent into a tissy by this revolutionist who can operate only where there are backward conditions. Take steps to alleviate the conditions, and Ché Djilas is sunk."

Andrew Wilkonson nodded again. "Perhaps ten years from now, yes."

"Why ten years? By that time Ché's movement might really be under way. These backward countries have to be aided into the era of the second industrial revolution."

"Very well. Listen for a moment. Shortly after the Second World War, Mr. Bader, large scale aid, so-called, was begun by the more advanced countries to the retarded ones. I am not referring to the Marshall Plan. Europe was already a developed area, it was simply in ruins, and all that was needed was American assistance to rebuild. But I refer to the so-called aid extended to the backward countries, especially by the United States and the Soviet Union. Arms, in particular, were exported to the value of billions of dollars and rubles. Even to such countries as those of Latin America where there hasn't been war for a century or more. To utilize your Yankeeism, they needed more arms like they needed a hole in the head. Many of the smaller wars fought about the globe at that time had both opponents armed with American weapons—supposedly aid.

"But that was not all. Usually, the provision was that the aid be spent in the country of its origin. So that if, say Argentina was awarded a loan of a hundred million, it had to be spent in the United States, where prices might be higher and often the materials purchased had to be transported in American bottoms, the most expensive in the world. The Russians, of course, made similar provisions, as did we of Europe, after our economies had recovered. Pray remember, too, that these were usually *loans*, not gifts, and there was interest attached. The country receiving the aid was obligated to repay it, with interest, which of course put added strains upon budgets already inadequate.

"It is not necessary to touch upon, at this time, some of the reality connected with the supposedly free military gifts. If you equip a nation with your military equipment, then their army is tied to you for replacements, ammunition, and so on. You give them the initial cannon, but the shells for it have to be purchased.

"On top of all else, the governments of these countries receiving aid were often dominated by the great powers supplying it and were often corrupt and often bloody stupid. The money received would be spent on, say, a national airline, for which they had little use. Or perhaps a great hydro-electric installation in a monstrously large dam. And when this great prestiguous affair was completed, it would be discovered that the country was too backward to utilize the power produced, and that the nearby land was not suitable for irrigation. Huge hospitals were sometimes built, only to discover that there were no trained doctors and nurses to staff them. I could think of a score of other examples."

"I don't believe I'm getting your point, Professor Wilkonson." Rex Bader was frowning.

"To be brutally frank, young man, the attempt to industrialize the backward nations was a farce."

Rex looked at him. "You mean it wasn't sincere?"

"I sometimes wonder. But sincere or not, it was fated to failure. The dream was, supposedly, to industrialize the whole world to the point that the advanced countries had achieved by the middle of the 20th Century. It was an impossible dream, at least at that time, and it is today. You see Mr. Bader, we do not now have available sufficient copper, lead, zinc and various other crucial raw materials to be able to industrialize the world. By the middle of the century, the United States was already utilizing more than fifty percent of all raw materials going into world industry. About 1950 she was the biggest exporter of copper in the world, ten years later she was the biggest importer. In the 19th Century, this country had literally mountains of the richest iron ore, but even mountains of ore play out eventually and she was forced to import from Venezuela, Labrador and elsewhere."

"I'm still not getting your point."

"Mr. Bader, if nations such as Venezuela, Chile, the Congo and the rest of the backward lands that supply the advanced nations with raw materials were to industrialize they would use their own copper, uranium, iron ore, agricultural products and so forth. And when they began to produce their own autos and other manufactured products, they would jolly well discontinue buying them from our countries. We would lose our sources of raw materials and our markets for manufactured goods as well."

Rex sat back in his chair. "Briefly, then, what it amounts to is that we advanced countries can't afford to have the less advanced catch up with us."

"That is correct."

"And that gives Ché Djilas his opening."

Wilkonson nodded. He said bitterly, "If we only had ten years. If we could just keep such as Ché Djilas off our backs for ten more years."

"What the hell would that do? It sounds to me that the guy's got a pretty saleable argument. The rich nations are getting richer and the poor ones are getting poorer, what with their large birth rate and all."

"We're not quite so cold blooded as what I have just said would indicate, Mr. Bader. Socioeconomics was an unknown field two centuries ago and largely so even one century ago. Today we can understand a bit more and hence plan economic developments. All the necessary scientific breakthroughs have been made, but technology trails behind science. We already have the laser-mole, for instance, but it will be five or ten years before we have really adapted it to full scale mining."

"The laser-mole?"

"Yes. Today, our deepest mines go down a mere 7,000 feet. The laser-mole, something like a submarine applied to land, rather than to the sea, would allow us to operate as much as five or ten miles deep and then we'd have all the raw materials we could use—for everybody. Men can't work that deep, of course, so the equipment will have to be automated, which is no problem.

"If that were not enough, we have in the near future, the mining of the sea. Per cubic mile the sea contains 150 million tons of solid matter, including almost all of the elements. The most abundant metal is magnesium which runs some 18 million tons but there are many others including about twenty tons of gold. And if that were not enough, consider that a hundred tons of igneous rock such as granite holds eight tons of aluminum, five of iron, and considerable amounts of titanium, chromium, nickel, copper, vanadium, tungsten and lead. With the advent of nuclear fushion power, both the sea and igneous rock become available for mining. Give us ten years and our technology will open all these sources for us, and world industrialization will become practical and there need no longer be under-developed countries. By that time too it is to be hoped that the great powers will have reached enough agreement to cooperate in helping our more unfortunate brothers, rather than in competing in our efforts to 'aid.'"

Rex Bader thought about it for long moments.

Finally he came to his feet. "Okay. I'll buy your story, Professor Wilkonson. Tomorrow I leave for Satellite City."

XIX

He retraced his route of a couple of weeks before, making no effort whatsoever to hide his identity, or anything else pertaining to the trip. He took public transportation to the American International Jetport off Long Island, and the Supersonic to the Mediterranean Jetport off Cannes, on the French Riviera. From there he took a local jet to Algiers and then a shuttle directly to Beni-Abbes. All along the way he made a point of watching expenditures.

At Beni-Abbes he had to spend the night before making his connections. He wished to leave on the same transport, the same day, to arrive at Satellite City at the same time. Part of his plan involved running into the same personnel. At the desk of the motel-type accommodations at Beni-Abbes, he made a point of requesting the most economical room available, which, on the face of it, was unusual in the facilities connected with the Satellite City Authority. In the restaurant, that night, he chose the least expensive of the meals on the elaborate menu.

In the morning, he presented himself at the reservation desk at the spaceport. One of the impossibly bright young things that were already irritating the bejazus out of him was there.

She said—brightly—"That will be five thousand pseudo-dollars, Mr. Bader. Or the equivalent in any currency you wish."

188

He said, "Well, what does that include?"

"Your round trip to Satellite City and your accommodations there for as long as you wish to remain." She seemed slightly taken back that he should ask. She said, "That is your room and meals. All else is extra."

"Don't I know it?" he said, as though unhappily.

She waited, there behind her desk, evidently expecting him to make the next move.

He said, "I have an account with the Satellite City Bank. Charge it to that."

"Oh, of course, Mr. Bader."

He said, "It might be under the name Harold Brown. Darned if I know."

She was not unaccustomed to multiple names, and beamed at him. "Of course Mr. . . . Brown."

"Bader," he said.

When he had gone, she flicked on one of the desk screens and said, "Mr. Rich, in Satellite City, please." And then, "Scrambled."

The trip to Satellite City was a duplication of his initial one, minus only the thrill of the first trip into space. He ascended the ramp which led to the passenger quarters of the space transporter nestled in the belly of the massive supersonic jet and allowed the efficient stewardess to strap him into the acceleration chair. This time, at least, he had no chattering companion to bend his ear. The chair next to him was vacant. In fact, there were only five other passengers. He wondered, vaguely, how many were needed for a trip to pay off. But then, of course, the space transporter carried freight as well.

The ground crew left, the stewardess buckled herself in and the light atop the pilot's cubicle burned *Take off of the Boostercraft*, and they were underway.

It went like clockwork. And evidently always did. If

there had ever been an accident to a space transporter heading for Satellite City, he had never heard of it. Possibly there had been in the earliest days of the project, but, if so, he hadn't read about it.

They reached the Satellite City dock and connected there the first pass. There was even less jockeying than before. The dock workers came in and the officer with the passenger list. Evidently, everyone was going to the orbital resort hotel. Their acceleration chairs were detached from the floor and they were pushed to the shuttlecraft which was to carry them to the hotel wheel.

The reception hall was as before. The girl at the desk, the same as the last time. She even remembered his name. "Welcome back to Satellite City, Mr. Brown."

"The name is Bader," he said, indicating it in the passenger list which the docking officer had put on the desk before her.

"Of course. The suite you had before is vacant, Mr. Bader. Would you like it again?"

He thought about it for a moment. "You know, I think I'd like to try one just a bit further in toward the hub, or whatever you call it, just to experience being in slightly less gravity."

"I could put you in just one level further. On the same level as the Galaxy Room."

"That would be fine," he told her. She said something into one of her desk screens and a small blonde came up, pert and fluffy.

However, still duplicating his first visit, one of the Protective officers approached. He said, "Sir, would you mind stepping into the office for a moment?"

Rex Bader frowned. "I can't imagine what for."

"Yes, sir," the other said politely.

Bader shrugged and followed him.

Not only was the cold eyed officer who had named himself Antony Berch there, but Al Rich as well. Berch came to his feet. Al Rich remained seated. For once, Rocky wasn't with him.

Berch said, "Ah, Mr. Bader, I thought I had made it clear the last time. . . ."

Scowling his puzzlement, Rex Bader opened his jacket to demonstrate that he was not wearing his shoulder rig gun harness.

Antony Berch turned his eyes toward the assistant who had brought Bader in. That worthy looked puzzled too.

"The scanner indicated more than the standard amount of metal, sir."

Rex Bader laughed. "Oh," he said. He reached into his pocket and brought forth the knife. "I don't know why I continue to carry this awkward thing. Pure habit, I guess."

Berch chuckled politely. "Oh yes, your pocket knife. Excuse us, Mr. Bader. Simply routine, of course. For your protection and everyone else's."

"Of course." He returned the knife to his pocket and turned to go.

Al Rich who had been eyeing him evenly, stood and said, "Just a moment, ah *Mister* Bader." There was a touch too much accent on the mister.

Rex Bader hesitated at the door. "Yes?"

Al Rich followed him out into the reception room and looked at him speculatively. He said, "I didn't exactly expect to see you again, Bader. What brings you to Satellite City this time?"

"The same thing that brings everyone else," Rex said.

Al Rich waited for him to go on.

"Sophia Anastasis let me know that Big Nick had deposited twenty-five thousand pseudo-dollars to my account here. There is exactly one place I can spend it without running afoul of the internal revenue people."

"You could transfer it to any bank on Earth," Rich said coldly.

"Not legally, I couldn't. The moment that money touches Earth, in any form, I'm legally required to pay taxes on it. It might take them a year, or twenty years to find out about it, but when they did it would be fraud and there's no time limit on fraud applying to income tax."

"So you came up here to blow it."

"Yes."

"How long do you plan on staying?"

"Until I've gambled it up, drank it up, or have gone through it by any other method you have of getting through the remaining twenty thousand pseudo-dollars."

"Suppose you win at your gambling, instead of losing?"

"In that unlikely case, I'd leave it on deposit here and take another vacation next year."

Al Rich thought about it. He wasn't particularly pleased. He said, "So you're not here on business this time?"

"That's right. I'm no longer in government employ."

"How did they react to your report?"

"Largely as could have been expected. Largely they accepted it."

Al Rich's attitude changed slightly. He said, "Well, we're here to show our guests a good time. Have one. Good luck in the casino. I understand you came out a little ahead, the last time."

"Thanks," Rex Bader said. He turned back to the little blonde who was to see him to his room.

She led him to an elevator bank and they took one up—he continued to think of it as up, rather than in—to the next level and down the corridor a short way to his suite, which was lettered R-2.

The interior was similar to, but not an exact duplicate of the one he had had before. The pseudo-windows portrayed different scenes and there would be no window set in the floor, but largely it was similar. He could barely notice the difference in gravity.

The girl chattered away, explaining the suite's workings.

He said, "Never mind, Miss. I've been here before." He looked at the autobar in the corner. "Oh, one thing. How much does a drink of, say, pseudo-whiskey cost on that thing?"

She seemed surprised. "Why, twenty-five dollars, I believe, Mr. Bader."

He hissed softly between his teeth. "Wow! I can see I'm not going to be doing much drinking if I'm going to stretch my money out."

It was probably, he realized, the first time the girl—the name Helen was stitched over her left breast—had ever heard any such comment in Satellite City. Any guest in Satellite City was automatically assumed to be so well-heeled that price was no object. Well, he had his image to maintain.

Helen left, rather precipitately, he thought. At least she hadn't given him the come-on that Gertrude had, on his first trip. It came to him that possibly all of the girls employed in Satellite City were available. If so, they were probably the most highly paid call girls in the history of the oldest profession. And if he was to continue his portrayal of a working man blowing some unexpected money, and stretching it as far as possible, he was going to have to steer clear. Such as Gertrude and Helen were millionaire's fare.

The door buzzed and he looked over at the identity screen. The face there was that of the cheerful Scoop Ericsson.

Rex opened up.

The publicity man said, "Oh. It's . . . Mr. Brown. I thought you were a newcomer. They gave me the name, uh, Rex Bader."

Rex went into his act. "Come on in. Come on in, Scoop. For once in your life, you can write something instead of erasing it."

The other looked at him strangely and entered.

He said, "How come the reversal of engines?"

Bader was off-hand. "The last trip was business. This one is pleasure. As a matter of fact, it wouldn't hurt me at all to have my name spread around a little in the news Earth-side. Sit down, Scoop."

The other took a chair and looked thirstily at the auto-bar. Rex Bader ignored that.

He settled into another chair and said, "The kind of people who can take vacations in Satellite City have a lot of pseudo-dollars to spread around. It wouldn't hurt me at all to get the reputation of being so successful that I can hang out in joints like this."

Scoop Ericsson said, "Well, fine. We can take a few pictures of you in the Galaxy Room, in the casino and so forth, and plaster them around down below. You know, the well-known Mr. Rex Bader, vacationing in Satellite City, resting from his exertions in the . . ." The publicity man looked at him. "Uh, what is your field, Mr. Bader?"

"I'm a private investigator." Rex chuckled. "I've been called the last of the private eyes."

"Private eye!"

"That's right. Private detective."

"Holy jumping saints! And you want me to let out the information that a private detective is here in Satellite City?"

"Why not? The publicity wouldn't hurt me. Build up my reputation."

"Couldn't hurt *you?* What do you think it would do to our clientel if they found out they were rubbing elbows with a private detective? You think they'd shallow that story that you were only here for a vacation?"

"Well, that's what I am here for."

"Sure, sure. It says here. Ha! Man, if the word went through this hotel that there was a private detective around, we'd lose half of our guests before the week was out. We'd lost 'em sooner but we don't have enough space transports to get them down fast enough. Holy jumping saints, friend, don't tell anybody your profession!"

The formerly easy-going newsman was aghast.

Rex Bader said, put off, "Well, I guess you know what you're talking about."

Scoop Ericsson stood and shook his head in despair. "I just got a new ulcer. Private investigator, in Satellite City. Oh, *noooooo.*"

Rex saw him to the door.

When the other was gone, he laughtd softly. He had a suspicion that before twenty-four hours had elapsed all the employees of the orbital resort hotel would know that he was a detective, on a vacation or no. And he wondered how many of the employees up here had criminal records. For all he knew Scoop himself was unable to return Earth-side. This must be the end of the line for many with international records with Interpol and other police organizations. Not that the Satellite City Authority would put up with psychopathic killers and such, but in the world as it has always been, there can be a narrow line between what is considered criminal and what is not, and the ability to wield money, or power, makes a great deal of difference.

Rex Bader moved over to the phone screen on the desk and activated it and said, "When I was here a couple of weeks ago under the name Harold Brown, I bought an evening suit. I left it and would like it now."

The face in the screen was distressed. "But, sir. If you left clothing here, it has been . . . disposed of."

"Like hell. That suit wasn't new when I bought it and when I left it wasn't thrown away. Not in this place. It doesn't make sense. Now, listen, I'm not on an expense account and I have to watch what I'm throwing away. I want that suit . . . or one just like it."

"A moment, sir."

XX

It was somewhat more than a moment, but not much more. Evidently, the Satellite City Orbital Resort Hotel did not make a policy of arguing with its guests. The suit, or one exactly like it, was delivered in the closet.

He took his time dressing and then picked up the little pamphlet which contained the charts of the public rooms and checked his position. The Galaxy Room was less than a hundred feet away. He put the pamphlet into the dress suit's inner jacket pocket and sauntered to the restaurant.

Warren, the *maitre d'* was there to greet him, but seemed a bit less affable than before. Rex Bader grinned inwardly. Had the word already gotten around that this guest was a misfit who couldn't be expected to tip and was too tight to spend lavishly on some of the more exotic services the hotel offered?

As before, the food was superlative and, as before, when it was through he made his way to the casino beyond. He noted the manner in which the doors automatically slid open for him as he approached. There was no identity screen, so evidently an electric eye was involved. Casually, he looked for it and located it. It was about four feet above the floor leel.

Inside, he glanced about the crowded gambling hall. Gina Angel, looking like one of her namesakes in a stunning evening dress with Balkan peasant motif, was at the nearest roulette wheel, playing intently. She didn't notice him enter.

Seymour Rice the Third did. He was sitting before a blackjack layout, looking impossibly gawky in his evening dress. Without doubt, the suit had been tailored by one of the most expensive houses available, but the freckled young redhead still looked as though he had slept in it. Well, that was of no importance. He was here and evidently had been accepted for what he in actuality was, the wealthy scion of a very wealthy family, and his monty was just as acceptable as that of the tin tycoon next to him, who wore his clothes as though he had been poured into them.

Rex Bader nodded to him, the merest flick of a nod and then turned immediately away. He had told the boy to stay clear of him until approached.

He went over to the cashier's stall and put his identity card phone in the slot. He said, "Ten hundred dollar chips, to be credited from my Satellite City account."

"Carried out, Mr. Bader," the screen told him and the chips tumbled into the silver bowl and once again he was reminded of a one armed bandit paying off.

Fiddling with the chips, he sauntered about the room, savoring the atmosphere of excitement which seems always to predominate in casinos. He wondered at people so wealthy that money could mean nothing to them. He projected an air of not being able to decide what game to settle upon, and finally wound up standing before the glassed over birdcage with its ten dice.

Antony Berch, done in evening clothes rather than uniform, was walking past. Evidently, when not employed in the reception room, when new guests were scheduled, he doubled as an attendant here in the casino.

He said, "I warned you it was a sucker-trap."

Rex grinned back, and said, "It's the prospect of that payoff that gets to me."

He put one of his chips in the slot and touched the button. The birdcage flipped over. Three sixes.

"See," Berch laughed before going on.

Rex Bader continued to take in the gambling device, a slight rueful smile twisting his lips.

A voice which he recognized, said from behind him, "You'll never learn. I told you that your chances of hitting on that thing are less than six hundred million to one."

He turned to face her and said, "Good evening, Miss Angel."

"I heard you had returned to spend your twenty-five thousand. So you don't have quite as much integrity as you boasted."

"That was before I had figured out how to spend it before the Internal Revenue boys took it away from me. How are you doing tonight?"

She grimaced and, on her, even a grimace looked good. "Terribly. I'm on my way for more chips."

He said, "It seems to me that it'd be something like perpetual motion. You draw your money out of the Satellite City Bank and bring it in here and play. If you win, you put it back in the bank. If you lose, the casino deposits the money in the bank which is actually your account. What's the point in going through the motions?"

She said, "It's the way I get all of my exercise," and left him.

He looked after her for a moment. She didn't have a figure like that through getting all her exercise in a gambling hall.

Then he looked back at the birdcage and put another of his white chips in the slot. He pushed the button.

The cage upended. Not a single six. He grunted self-deprecation.

Gina Angel came up with a double handful of blue chips. She said, as though taking pity on him, "Come along. I'm going to change my luck by switching to *The Escargot* system."

He followed her to a different roulette wheel than the one at which she had been stationed before. There were fewer persons about this one, seven or eight. He took his place next to her, scarcely looking at the others.

"*The Escargot?*" he said.

"Yes. Now watch how I do this. You bet one chip on a one to one payoff, like odd or even, or black or red, and continue at that rate until you lose, at which time you write down the number one on a piece of paper." She indicated the pads of paper and the pencils which were scattered about the table for the benefit of players who were working systems.

It came to Rex Bader even as he concentrated on what she was telling him, that the tall man directly across from him was vaguely familiar.

Gina Angel was saying, "You then bet two chips and continue to bet two as long as you continue losing. The moment you win, you cross off your first number on the paper and write down two and play three chips until you win again. And so on. Figure it out and you'll find that with this system even if you lose five bets and win five bets you will still be five chips ahead."

"Devil take it," Rex said. Using her system, he began to bet on odd. She stuck to red. But something was nagging at him. Surreptitiously he looked at the dapper tall man across the way.

Then it came to him. It was the other's somewhat indolent stance that he seemed to recognize. The face was that of a complete unknown. And then his eyes locked for the briefest of moments with those of the other. The face was that of a complete unknown, but the stone-hard eyes were those of Colonel Ilya Simonov and there was a wolfish gleam in them.

Gina Angel was muttering bitterly under her breath. While Rex Bader was winning, using her system, she was just as consistently losing.

Finally she swore under her breath in a most unladylike way and said, "I'm going for more chips."

Rex Bader grinned at her and said, "Perpetual motion. Think of all the money the casino is making tonight. You'll find it in your account in the morning."

"Shut up," she hissed and grinned back.

Ilya Simonov had been playing a group of four numbers, 14, 15, 17 and 18 and continuing to lose. He came around the table and stood next to Rex Bader.

"You seem to be the only one here who wins," he growled ungraciously.

Bader pretended to ignore the ill humor. He said, "This system is too slow. I think I'll play a hunch. My suite is R-2. On this table, number two is red. In short, R-2. How can I lose?"

The other looked at him in the repulsion dedicated gamblers have for the hunch player and said nothing further.

Rex played the number two and lost. Played again and lost, and then, in seeming disgust took up his chips. He left the roulette wheel and went back to the birdcage and stared at it as though in frustration.

Another player came up and said, "I beg your pardon. If you don't mind?" He indicated the chip he held in his hand.

Rex Bader growled, "I'm playing it." And put in a

chip. He pushed the button. The cage flipped over. One six.

The stranger stood there patiently.

Rex put another chip in. Two sixes. Another. No sixes at all.

Gina Angel came up to his side and looked at him as though he was an idiot. "Good heavens are you insane? This is a trick. A gag. It's just for laughs. You can't win."

He glared at her. "You mean it's rigged?"

"No, of course not. It's absolutely on the up and up, but there has never been a gambling game in history with that bad a percentage. It's worse than a lottery. It's worse than the old policy numbers racket used to be. Don't be a fool . . . Rex."

He put one more chip in. Four sixes.

"That's the best I've done so far," he grumbled.

She snorted contempt and headed for the roulette wheel, as though giving him up as a lost cause.

He jiggled his chips in his right hand. He counted them and scowled. He put one more in the slot. Not even one six turned up out of the ten. He grumbled anger and left.

He drifted about the room, stopping occasionally at this game or that, kibitzing, but not playing. His humor was obviously sour. Sometimes he would watch for several minutes, then he'd drift on again.

He came up behind Seymour Rice who was still at his blackjack game and was evidently winning a little. There was no one else at the blackjack layout.

Rex Bader said, without moving his lips. "Suite R-2, on this floor, four o'clock in the morning."

Seymour Rice stiffened infinitesimally and ran a hand through his red hair, but didn't turn. Rex Bader drifted off. After a few minutes he returned to the birdcage and

202

stood there and stared at it, while two others came up and gave the device a try. Neither of them achieved more than two sixes.

When they were gone, Rex put two more chips into the slot, doing no better than they had.

The girl named Gertrude, who had first played bellhop for him, came by, charmingly done in a shorty evening gown. She said, in amusement, "You dreamer, you," and continued on her way.

He looked down at his remaining chips. He had exactly ten, the number with which he had begun the evening. He put them all into the slot, one after the other, all ten, and with the same result he had been getting all evening.

He glared at the machine as though about to assault it, then turned on his heel and marched from the casino.

He returned to his suite and dialed a drink, a pseudo-whiskey and soda, on the autobar. When it came, he took it into the bath and poured it into the wash basin.

Ht sat down in one of the comfort chairs and checked out the hotel pamphlet and the various entertainment it listed. He came upon what he was looking for and dialed the appropriate number. The ultra-pornagraphic show began to flash on the Tri-Di screen which occupid a sizeable portion of one wall.

He didn't bother to watch. Vicarious sex had never appealed to him. After a few minutes he went over to the autobar and dialed another pseudo-whiskey. When it came, he took it into the bathroom and poured it away, as he had the first.

He had hardly reseated himself than a gentle knock came at the door.

It was Ilya Simonov, in his new appearance. He was

203

standing to the side of the door so that he wouldn't be picked up by the identity screen. Rex Bader let him in, then went over and switched off the Tri-Di.

The espionage chief held a finger to his lips and brought forth from a pocket the electronic device he had told Bader, once before, was a scrambler. He let his eyebrows go up in question.

Rex shook his head. "No bugs in Satellite City."

"How can you be sure?"

"It's the only thing that makes sense. The people who patronize Satellite City do not want bugs, period. Nor anything else that intrudes on privacy. That's what they sell here, complete privacy, and they'd be fools to do differently."

"They could claim to deliver that, but in actuality——"

Bader was shaking his head. "No. There are hundreds of maintenance people, hotel employees, orbital hospital employees, science technicians and all the rest of them, up here. One man can keep a secret, two don't do it so well. When you get hundreds of people who might stumble on your secret, it stops being a secret. One sorehead could blow the whistle on you. If the word got out that the orbital hotel had electronic bugs around—even one —then hundreds of the permanent guests, not to speak of the transitory ones, would take off like lemmings. No. There are no bugs in Satellite City. No monitoring of conversations, or anything remotely resembling it."

He smiled ruefully, "Besides, I've checked out the whole project. I've had experts check it out. We've gone through all the plans, checked all the sophisticated equipment that's gone into the whole city. There *are* no bugs up here."

Simonov nodded. "Very well, I'll have to take your assumption. Admittedly, I had already come to the same conclusion."

He took a chair.

Rex Bader said, "Okay. Great. What in the hell are you doing here?"

Now that he was looking at the other more closely, he could see that the disguise was not cosmetic surgery but a very clever altering of the features by what must have been false teeth which changed the shape of the jaw, by probably plugs in the nostrils, possibly injections of some sort of sponge-like plastic material into the neck to make it larger.

Ilya Simonov said easily, "I came to help you."

"And took the chance of blowing my cover?"

"You've been clever enough to utilize practically no cover at all, which astonishes me." He hesitated. "In fact, so far as I can see, you have no cover."

"I don't need any. But how about you? Sophia Anastasis, at least, is aware of you, Colonel. And she knows that you were at that meeting in Harrington's offices in the Octagon."

"My cover goes back the better part of a century, Mr. Bader. And this is far from the first time I have been a guest in Satellite City."

"Century?" Rex said blankly.

"Briefly, in 1917 General Alexis Yaroslavl managed to escape the revolution through Vladivostok. With him were the jewels of his wife, the Princess Natalie who had been caught by the Bolsheviks and, ah, liquidated. He managed to get first to Paris, later to London. The jewels were rivaled only by those of the Romanoffs and were worth millions. He sold them, invested the proceeds, and refrained from spending them. He was waiting to donate the money to the cause, when the White Armies attempted to restore Czardom. However, he was an old man, Mr. Bader. When his son, the Count Nicolas, supposedly escaped from the Reds, he turned the fortune's administration over to him, not knowing that the young count was a passionate follower of Lenin. Nicolas continued to invest the fortune, even after his father's death, and increased it considerably. In turn, upon his demise, the fortune, now invested in a score of countries, was turned over to his son."

Ilya Simonov came to his feet, clicked his heels, bowed from the waist. "Meet Count Pavel Yaroslavl, the multimillionaire playboy, known everywhere, but everywhere, as the last of the Russian big spenders, come down from the old Imperial days."

Rex Bader stared at him. "Holy Moses, but you're the field head of the *Chrezvychainaya Komissiya*."

"That is correct, Comrade Bader, and also, under a different pseudonym, the pretender to the Czar's throne, since the demise of the late Grand Duke Dimitri. Believe me, the Soviet Complex is thorough in its espionage-counter-espionage."

XXI

Rex Bader said, "Talk about *cover*. But why tell me?"

Simonov sat again. "To gain your confidence by baring my all," he said blandly. "I'm here to help. Things are coming to a head. There have been riots in Santos and Rio de Janeiro in favor of Ché Djilas' movement. In the American Senate, hotheads have accused the Soviet Complex of sponsoring Djilas and have called for increased armaments. Admittedly, so far, these have come from the States that would profit most from an arms race. However, more Djilas success and who knows what others would jump on the anti-Soviet bandwagon? Changes are being made in our part of the world, Bader, and at this point we can't afford a new arms race—if we ever could. We're clutching at straws. We are desperate. We want Djilas eliminated. You evidently have some sort of plan which you think will work. Very frankly, all of my own plans have come a cropper, to use your Yankeeism. Can I help?"

Bader looked at him thoughtfully. He stood and went to the autobar and dialed another pseudo-whiskey. When it came, he repeated his process of taking it into the bath and pouring it away.

He came back to his visitor. "Yes," he said. "You can. I can use a lookout. The first stage of the scheme is set for tonight at four a.m. Meet here. Try not to be seen in the corridors, although there's practically nobody in them at that time. If you are seen, look as though you're strolling aimlessly, as though you haven't been able to get to sleep."

"Can you tell me the basic plan? I haven't been able to figure out a way of getting him out of Satellite City, even if I could locate him."

"No."

The other nodded. "Very well. I'll be here." He stood and looked at Rex Bader to see if there was anything more. There evidently wasn't, so he left.

About half an hour later, Rex Bader repeated his routine with the drinks. And once again at mid-night, this time ordering two at once. At two o'clock, he ordered a bottle, poured half of it away, and left the balance sitting on a side table.

Seymour Rice the Third, turned up first, a few minutes before four. His youthful, less than handsome face was nervous in the identity screen. In fact, his Adam's apple bobbed twice. Rex opened up and let him in.

"Anybody see you come here?"

"I don't think so. What are we going to do?"

"I'll tell you later. I don't want to upset you, prematurely."

Exactly at four, there came a tap at the door. It was Colonel Ilya Simonov, of course. Rex let him in. The Colonel looked at Seymour Rice, obviously surprised.

Rex said, "There is no need for you two to know each other. Let's go. We'll try and avoid anyone seeing us. It shouldn't be difficult at this hour. If we do see anybody, pretend to be slightly drunk, as though we were returning from a late party."

They nodded. Seymour Rice gulped, his Adam's apple bobbing.

They ran into no one whatsoever in the hundred feet or so to the Galaxy Room. The doors were closed, but, as Rex Bader knew, there was no lock.

He looked at the Russian espionage man. "Go in and see if there is anyone inside. A clean-up man, or whatever. If there is, pretend that you thought the restaurant was open all night. Pretend you're drunk. Then we'll have to figure out some way of getting rid of him. Possibly you can insist he see you back to your quarters. That would take enough time for what we two have to do."

Simonov nodded and pushed his way into the dining room. He came out within seconds and shook his head.

Bader said, "Okay, quickly," to young Rice and they entered.

The Galaxy Room's lights were dim and the luxurious and ornate atmosphere strangely depressing without its laughing and talking clientele, its scurrying captains and waiters, its muted music.

Rex Bader led the way. When they were within a few yards of the casino doors he turned to Ilya Simonov. He said, "Now this is the crucial point. We can't be disturbed. If somebody enters the restaurant here while we're inside, you've got to figure out some way of disposing of him. We shouldn't be more than about ten minutes."

Simonov nodded and twisted his solid shoulders beneath his jacket as though in preparation for action.

Rex Bader brought forth his fancied-up pocket knife from his trousers pocket and got down on his hands and knees and crawled to the door, avoiding the electric eye. He didn't know whether or not it was activated but he didn't want to take any chances. He reached up with the knife and pushed the stud set in its side, the way they had taught him in John Mickoff's so-called Department of Dirty Tricks. The door clicked.

He said over his shoulder to Seymour Rice, "Come on, down on your knees the way I am." He slid the doors back.

Rice followed him into the casino, crawling. Rex Bader closed the door behind them and came to his feet. He brought an envelope from his pocket and extracted from it the syrette that Professor Moselle had given him. Seymour Rice understood, gulped and bobbed his Adam's apple and bared his arm. Bader injected him.

He said, "Over here," and led the youth to the bird-cage. He pointed at the ten dice. "I want you to turn them over, all ten, so that sixes are uppermost."

"It'll be a few minutes before the booster works."

"Okay. Take your time."

"You're sure this is of national importance to the United States of the Americas?"

"Yes. I'll give you the details some day when we've returned Earth-side. Right now, it's better if you don't know."

Seymour Rice hunkered down awkwardly on his heels so as to be nearer to the birdcage bottom and the dice in it. Blisters of sweat began to appear on his forehead. He began to stare, demonically.

One of the dice began to stir a trifle. Rex Bader took in a deep breath. The die turned over, bringing a four to the top. It stirred again, turned again. A six was uppermost now. Seymour Rice turned his attention to the next one. The sweat was rolling from him now and his eyes were popping. Lon Chaney playing *The Wolf Man* came to Bader's mind.

When all ten of the dice read six up, Seymour Rice

giggled. He brought a handkerchief from his pocket and mopped his face.

A voice from behind them said softly, "What in the hell's going on here?"

Rex Bader spun. It was Rocky and he had obviously entered the casino from a door other than the one to the Galaxy Room where Simonov stood guard.

The chunky, evasive eyed guard came up smoothly and stared at the birdcage and then at Rex Bader and his younger companion.

"I'll be damned," Rocky grinned. "Figured out some way of gimmicking it, eh?" He held his head back and laughed delight. "I had a funny feeling something was up. You know the way you get those funny feelings sometimes? Well, I'll be damned."

Rex Bader was on him.

Rocky met him with a pile hammer of a fist straight to the heart. Rex swung, left, right, left to the face. The professional bodyguard tucked his chin into his left shoulder and grinned even as he reached out his own left, connecting brutally.

Rex Bader shuffled three steps back and snapped to the wide-eyed Seymour Rice, "Get Simonov. Quick."

The youngster didn't know the name, but he immediately realized who Bader was obviously talking about. He giggled and scooted for the door, getting down on hands and knees to go through.

Rocky's eyes narrowed and he shot a look at the door for which Seymour Rice was heading, and then another at the far end of the hall from which he had entered. He obviously came to the conclusion that his best bet was to drum up some help. He couldn't know how much assistance was on the way for Bader.

He came boring in, trying for a quick elimination of

his present opponent, his fists a blur of speed. Rex Bader met him, blow for agonizing blow. They were both panting and groaning, like a couple of pugs on a Tri-Di show. Rex Bader could feel himself weakening. The other was granite hard, fast as a cougar and fighting his own style.

His downfall was through triple cause. First, he had defeated this Rex Bader once before and was hence overly confident of being able to take him again. Second, he was in too much of a hurry to finish the other off and depart the room. He wasn't quite sure what was up, but he knew it was something big and he couldn't run the risk of staying and fighting at least three men, even though one was hardly more than a boy. Third, he heard someone at the door behind him, and made the mistake of turning for a quick glance.

Rex Bader's fist hit him full in the throat. The heavier man staggered back, gasping in pain and for breath. Bader moved in in a flurry of blows as he delivered the remaining of his strength. One, two, three, four.

Suddenly, he could hit no more. Rex stepped backward panting his exhaustion. Rocky, reeling, fell forward on one knee. He caught his breath and began to stagger erect, back to his feet. Was the man indestructable?

Colonel Ilya Simonov came up behind him and chopped him in the back of the neck with the side of his hand. The snap of the spine was clearly audible. Rocky collapsed forward.

Rex stood there, breathing in gasps. The action had been as fast as any he had ever been in. Simonov looked down at the dead man, then up at Rex.

He said, "What effect has this on your scheme?"

"Bad."

"Otherwise, how was it going?"

"Successfully. Practically a sure thing . . . I think. But I need at least until noon tomorrow to finish. I should have Djilas by then."

Seymour Rice had also returned on hands and knees, having the presence of mind to close the door to the Galaxy Room restaurant behind him. He stared down at the body in sick fascination and then, incongruously, giggled.

Bader said, "If he's found, particularly here, the fat is in the fire. We wouldn't have a chance."

The colonel thought about it. "There's a disposal unit in the Galaxy Room kitchens. They eject things out into spact with a very small rocket to boost it away from the city. They don't reutilize quite *everything* up here."

Young Rice stuttered, "You've got to have a spacesuit to go into the unit. I . . . I took a guided tour the other day. They showed us." He giggled uncontrollably.

Simonov looked at him, and then at Bader. "What's the matter with him?"

"After-effects of a drug I had to give him. He's got to get into bed soon. I'll take him back to my room and take care of him. I've already got an alibi in the making. Probably won't need it, but just in case."

The colonel nodded. "Very well, Bader. I'll see that our friend, here, is kept out of the way until at least noon tomorrow."

"What are you going to do?"

"It's not important," the other grinned wolfishly. "I'm expendable." He stopped and, as though effortlessly, took up the dead man and slung him over his shoulder.

All right, Rex Bader decided, that part of it was the colonel's top, let him spin it. Bader turned and took Seymour Rice by the arm and led him toward the Galaxy

Room and the corridor beyond, making him crawl again as they went under the electronic eye. He closed the doors behind him, and relocked them.

They were nearly to his suite before they passed anyone. It was a uniformed maintenance man, obviously on a night shift. He looked at them questioningly. The boy was seemingly drunk. Rex managed a bit of staggering himself.

He said, "Merry Christmas."

The man said, "Yes, sir," and passed on.

In the suite again, Rex Bader poured the young ESP expert onto the couch in the living room, went over to the autobar and ordered two drinks. When they arrived, he took one over to the young Rice who was now deep in sleep. The after effects of the psychodelic drug, or whatever it was, seemed to have hit him sooner this time. Bader poured the drink over his companion's clothes and put the glass next to him. He swallowed half of the other drink and poured the second half onto the rug. He dropped the glass and broke it. Then he went into the bathroom and collected up the earlier glasses he had ordered before the expedition to the casino, and put them around the room haphazardly.

He stood in the middle of the suite and looked about and finally nodded. It looked as though one hell of a drinking binge had taken place. He went over to the autobar again and ordered one last drink. This one, he took down. He wanted the smell of liquor on his breath in the morning.

XXII

At nine thirty, the next day, he called Service on the phone screen on the desk and slurred his voice. "I gotta friend here, passed out last night in my suite. Name's . . . less see. Name's Rice, I think he said. Can you send somebody, take him to his own place? I don't even know what suite he's in."

He shook the boy awake. Seymour Rice seemed reasonably his old self, though a little bleary of eye.

Rex Bader said urgently, "They're sending somebody to get you back to your suite. Pretend you have one hell of a hangover. When you get back there, make immediate plans to return Earth-side. Don't communicate with me any further. I'll see you in Southern University City. And thank you—from me and the government of your country, Mr. Rice."

When the other was gone, escorted most politely by two of the bright young things, as though this was an absolutely everyday occurrence, Rex Bader got his jacket and headed for the casino.

The Galaxy Room was not set up at ten o'clock in the morning. Evidently guests took their breakfasts either in their suites or in one of the other restaurants. However, there was passage to the casino for those who wished to gamble in the morning.

Rex Bader was the first to enter, although others straggled in almost immediately after. He knew the type. The old diehards, usually elderly women, bejeweled, over-dressed, and inch deep in cosmetics which made them hard and tough in appearance, rather than youthful. They were the type to be seen in the casinos around the world. They entered at opening and usually had a favorite chair which they invariably occupied. They carried their own pads of paper with which to work out their systems or utilized those that the house provided. They were the serious gamblers. Not for them such nonsense as the birdcage with its impossible odds. Rex Bader knew that there was little need for worrying that any of them would approach that device, stationed so prominently in the dead center of the gambling hall.

Antony Berch was standing at the door when it opened at exactly ten o'clock. He smiled at Rex, took in his somewhat bedraggled appearance and came to the obvious conclusions. The other had been drunk the night before.

"Good morning, Mr. Bader," he nodded. "How was your luck, last night?"

"Awful," Rex Bader grumbled ungraciously. "Made a little at roulette and dropped it all in that damned bird-cage."

Berch looked politely sorrowful. "As I told you, sir, it's not a serious way of gambling."

"It's pretty damn serious when you drop a couple of thousand pseudo-dollars into it," Bader growled, going on by.

He went to the auto-cashier and got his usual ten white chips and then sauntered over to the blackjack layout at which Seymour Rice had been sitting the night before. He stared at it glumly, as though trying to decide whether or not to play. It was the closest table to the birdcage. He didn't expect anyone else to approach that

216

device for awhile, but he couldn't take any chances. He had to get there first.

Others were streaming in, most of them making a beeline for roulette, baccarat or Chemin de Fer tables. He had to take care now. He needed plenty of witnesses, but he mustn't, mustn't, mustn't let anybody get to that birdcage first.

He noticed Scoop Ericsson enter and drift about. Good. Couldn't be better. And then, to his surprise, Sophia Anastasis. She bought herself a stack of blue chips, then noticed him and came over, on the way to one of the roulette wheels.

As gorgeous as ever in a trim morning suit, she looked him up and down appraisingly. "I heard you were here. So you decided to use the twenty-five thousand on sampling the . . . ah, good life, after all." She lifted a corner of her mouth at the term *good life*. On the face of it, Miss Anastasis thought the orbiting resort hotel a sucker trap for the well heeled.

Rex Bader said, "You seem to enjoy an occasional fling here yourself."

"Fling?" she snorted. "I'm here on business." She swept on by.

He couldn't put it off any longer. There were already at least fifty players in the room. He went over to the birdcage and scowled at it sourly. He looked over at Antony Berch, still at the door. Berch smiled and shook his head negatively. Rex Bader grunted and turned back to the machine which, seemingly, hypnotically fascinated him.

So far as he could see, there was only one table the occupants of which, if they looked in this direction, might be able to see the cage flip over. He moved around so that his back shielded the device from the potential eyes.

He brought forth one of his white chips and pretended to insert it. And pretended to touch the button.

And yelled at the top of his voice, *"YOWEE!"*

All eyes goggled at him. For some unknown reason, the habitues of gambling casinos seemed inclined to low voices. Antony Berch came hurrying over, as though Bader had suddenly slipped over the edge, or was drunk or something, and would have to be escorted from the hall before he bothered the other guests further.

He came up, his attitude still differential and began to say, "My dear, Mr. Bader . . ."

Then his eyes popped. He stared unbelievingly at the ten sixes. His jaw dropped open.

He said, "Holy Mother."

Silence fell throughout the casino, as though suddenly, intuitively, everyone present knew what had happened. Then there were squeals, the scraping of chairs being pushed back. A scramble to hurry to the spot.

"Oh God," a woman shrilled. "And I was just about to come over and try it." She rolled her eyes upwards and fell back into the arms of the man behind her in a full faint.

Suddenly, pushing his way through the crowd, Al Rich materialized. His face was aghast.

He got out, "I don't believe it! It's a trick!"

A fat man said shrilly, "Don't believe it? Don't believe it? There they are, ten sixes. For years we've been dropping hundred dollar chips into that damned thing and now finally it hits and you refuse to pay off!"

There were other voices of indignation.

Al Rich held up his hands, which were shaking. "Please, please, everyone. As you all know, the Satellite City Authority always pays off. Our reputation is at stake." His face was as drained as death.

Scoop Ericsson pounded Rex Bader on the back. Rex had been standing through all this as though struck speechless after his initial shout. Scoop yelped, "How about that! Now this is what I call publicity! Ha! Every news media in the world will carry it. One-hundred-million-pseudo-dollars to the lucky man who decided to take a chance in the Satellite City casino!"

Al Rich looked at him in loathing. "Shut up," he said. "I've got to think." He turned back to Rex Bader, his face still ashen. He said, "Obviously, Mr. Bader, the casino does not have such a sum on hand immediately. Would you mind accompanying me to the offices to make arrangements?"

"Course not," Bader told him, as though trying to keep his voice off hand. Grinning at the crowd which was packed deep about the birdcage, he followed the orbital hotel manager. To his relief, he noted that already others were pressing in to play against the heavy odds. They had witnessed that the birdcage could be beaten and were in there anxious to try. The ten sixes were now but a memory, but Rex Bader had half a hundred of the world's most wealthy gamblers to witness that he had made it.

Al Rich looked at Antony Berch and gestured with his head. The Protective officer followed them. They filed out of the casino and headed for the bank of elevators in the Galaxy Room. Evidently, the word was already going around. Dozens of guests were streaming for the gambling hall. What they expected to see there, Rex Bader couldn't figure out. The ten sixes were long since gone.

While they waited for an elevator, Al Rich said to Berch. "Have you seen Rocky? He was supposed to keep an eye on this character."

Berch shook his head. "No, Mr. Rich."

Bader looked at the Satellite City official. "What do you mean, character? I'm an honored guest of this establishment."

"We'll see about that," Rich said grimly.

They took the elevator inward toward the axis and Rex Bader assumed that he knew their destination. And he was right. They emerged on a level with approximately one quarter gravity and again he had to watch his footing, though the other two were used to it.

And again they were confronted with the disagreeable Dominick who shook them all down as before. This time he was even more careful with Rex Bader and came up with the pocket knife.

He took Bader in with his small, hard gray eyes and said, "What's this?"

Al Rich said impatiently, "It's his pocket knife. He says he's been carrying it since he was a boy scout, or something."

Dominick said, "I'll just hold onto it while you're with Mr. Mangano."

Rex shrugged, as though he couldn't care less.

They entered the living room, office combination of Nicolo Mangano. It could have been as though the last occasion during which he had been present had happened only moments before. Emanuele, the secretary, was behind his utilitarian metal desk; Big Nick, seemingly dressed exactly the same as before, in spite of the humid intense heat of the room, behind his. To complete the tableau, Gina Angel drifted in from a back room.

For a long moment, Big Nick, only his large eyes alive in his sallow gray face, stared at the newcomers. The news had already undoubtedly been sent up to him.

Rex Bader found himself a chair, crossed his legs and

said to Gina Angel. "Well, you were wrong. The birdcage finally lost."

She cocked her head and snorted softly, "Did it?"

Big Nick looked at her. "*Tesoro mio*, whats'a percent on thata machine?" He let his sagging eyelids close over his eyes while he listened.

She snorted contempt. "There is none. Over six hundred million to one."

Mangano said, after breathing deeply once or twice, "Al, how many times the marks play thata machine?"

"Maybe a hundred a night, Nick. A take of ten thousand."

"So, in a years'a time, maybe t'irty thousand marks, they'sa try it, hah?" He looked over at Emanuele. "How many years at thata rate, she'sa take before the percent say she'sa hit?"

Emanuele looked blank. "Why, hundreds, sir."

Gina laughed softly. "Thousand, Nick. Forever. That birdcage's just a gag. Kind of a publicity stunt. Anybody who's ever heard of the Satellite City casino knows there's a birdcage that pays off a million to one."

Rex Bader said softly, "Nevertheless, the ten sixes came up."

Sophia Anastasis, as cool and collected as always, entered the door by which Rex and his escort had come in earlier. She nodded at her associates and found a chair without saying anything.

Antony Berch said in agitation, "I saw him do it."

All eyes went to him.

But it was Sophia Anastasis who shook her head and said gently, "No you didn't, you clod. You didn't even go over to him, until he yelled."

And the eyes went to her.

221

She said softly, "I suppose I was the only one to actually be looking at him, at the time. He went through all the motions, as though he was putting a chip in the slot, then as though he was pushing the button. But the cage didn't flip."

Rex Bader said, with his slightly rueful smile, "Nevertheless, there are more than fifty of your highly placed guests down there, Miss Anastasis, who saw the ten sixes. So obviously, you're mistaken."

Al Rich had regained a modicum of collection. He snapped, "He's found some way of gimmicking it. Any gambling machine ever invented can be gimmicked. I'll send it over to the science wheel. They've got some men over there that'll find out how it was done. If we can prove a crooked deal, we won't have to pay off."

Rex Bader looked at him. "They won't find anything, Rich. I can guarantee you that." His eyes went back to Sophia Anastasis. "Even if you were correct, Miss Anastasis, that I had figured out some fancy way of getting around the birdcage, you'd still have to pay off. Fifty people saw the ten sixes. By this time, everybody in the hotel knows about them. Within a few days, everyone in the world will know about it. You're not going to convince them that it wasn't on the up-and-up. And what happens if the casino doesn't pay off? How much confidence will your customer have in your Satellite City Bank and your Bourse? How many of your scientists, over in the Science Wheel, will disaffiliate themselves from you in disgust? How many of those patients over in the hospital wheel will continue to leave sizeable fortunes to the Authority when they find out it welches?"

Al Rich said dangerously, "You're taking a lot of chances, aren't you Bader?"

Rex Bader shook his head at him. "I doubt it. I'm safe

from violence from you people. If anything happened to me, either here or down Earth-side, the whole world would point its finger at you. They'd *know* you had done it. They'd look into the Satellite City ownership and discover that it's in the hands of what we once called the Mafia. A real stink would go up. In actuality, it would behoove you people to put bodyguards on me, just to be sure that some other violence, from some other source, never happened to me. Because if something did, you'd get the blame."

A screen on Emanuele's desk hummed and he answered it and looked up and said, "It's for you, Mr. Rich."

Al stood and bent over the screen.

When he looked up again, his face was empty. "It's Rocky," he said. "They've found him outside—without a spacesuit."

Gina Angel shook her head in rejection, sick. "How . . . how . . ."

"They don't know yet. Just floating around out there. Along with one of the guests, that big spending Russian, Count Yaroslavl." Al Rich came slowly around to Bader. "You bastard. I had Rocky keeping an eye on you."

"What am I supposed to say to that? Do I look like I could heave that over-grown ape out into space? Not to speak of somebody else to keep him company. I wouldn't know how to go about it, even if I could."

Big Nick opened his eyes. His thick gray tongue came out and licked his shrunken lips. "It'sa too bad about Rocky, but he was'a nothing but a punk. Let'sa get back to thisa one hundred million, hah? There'sa lot'sa funny thing happen aroun' here, hah? For me, Big Nick, it'sa funny this'a happen to you, Mr. Bader. Alla people come up here and for years they'sa play this crazy machine no-

223

body could possible hit. But you, a private eye, come up here firsta time lookin' for trouble. Second time you come up, you hit it right off, Mr. Bader. It'sa kinda funny."

"It's not important," Rex said mildly. "I don't figure on collecting it. I don't want the hundred million."

If he'd pulled a gun and started shooting, he couldn't have gotten to them more effectively. Even the ever poised Sophia Anastasis gaped, even the sauve Al Rich bug-eyed.

Big Nick came up with the nearest thing to a blurted sentence of which his frail body was capable. "What'sa matter with you, hah? You crazy?"

"No. Suppose I took it. I'd be in the ninety-five percent bracket. Internal Revenue would take ninety-five million as a beginning."

Gina Angel said, in amusement, "You could go to India, Mr. Bader, and, ah, hunt Bengal Tigers in comfort for the rest of your years, with or without twenty-two pistols."

"And have Internal Revenue waiting for me for the rest of my life. Suppose they cooked up some extradition laws with India, for tax evaders? Or suppose India had a revolution and confiscated my money? Then I'd be on the run and never be able to go back to my own country, the one country in which I'd like to live, or the revenue boys would have me. No thanks, I'd rather not break the laws."

Angel said, frowning slight puzzlement. "But suppose you went back to the States and paid the tax; you'd still have five million."

"Okay. And your animosity for the rest of my life. You people think I've pulled a quick one. I have an idea that your organization has patience, both Diversified Industries and the Satellite City Authority. Possibly you're willing to wait for twenty years, when everybody has forgotten my good luck, to have your revenge. Possibly you have other ways to get at me. Like lousing up any investment I might make with my five million. No thanks. I'd rather make a deal, in return for the hundred million."

"A deal, hah? What'sa this'a deal, Mr. Bader," Big Nick got out. He brought forth a clean handkerchief from a drawer and swabbed his forehead. He was sweating, but the impression was that he was cold, cold. He looked at Gina. "Gina, *cara mia,* you get Mr. Bader a drink, hah?"

While Gina sauntered over to the bar, not bothering to ask for preferences, Rex Bader looked full into the face of Nicolo Mangano.

"I want you to turn Ché Djilas over to me."

XXIII

Big Nick took the time to catch his breath. Finally, he said, "Who'sa this Ché Djilas?"

Rex Bader stared at him. He said impatiently, "I'm playing this straight with you, Mr. Mangano. Give me Ché Djilas and I'll pretend to the world news media, and all, that you paid off the one hundred million."

The Syndicate head looked at Al Rich. "Who'sa this Ché Djilas who'sa worth a hundred million?"

Al Rich stiffened. His mouth worked. He didn't seem to be able to get out words.

Sophia Anastasis took the ball. "There isn't any such person, Uncle Nick. He is supposed to be a kind of communist of the old school, down on Earth. But there isn't any such person."

"The hell there isn't," Rex Bader growled. "And what's more he's gone to ground here in Satellite City." He turned back to Nick Mangano. "My government wants him, Mr. Mangano. And so do half the other legitimate governments in the world. I'm willing to trade him for the hundred million."

Big Nick said, "There'sa somthin' goin' on aroun' here Big Nick he don' like." He said, without looking at them, "Antony, Emanuele, you getta out."

The two underlings got.

Gina Angel handed the long cool drink to Rex Bader,

giving him a wink in passing. "Good heavens," she murmured to him. "But you do cause trouble."

He took a long draught thankfully. His body was running sweat again. The rest of them must have been used to Big Nick's quarters and to its impossible heat.

Mangano looked at Sophia Anastasis and Al Rich. "Okay. Now we'sa fin' out about thisa Ché Diljas. Or maybe I hafta call in Tony and Salvatore, hah?"

Al Rich said, "Now, look, Nick . . ."

But Sophia Anastasis, considerably more collected, took over. "See here, Uncle Nick, this is an Earth-side operation we've taken on. We didn't figure it applied to Satellite City."

"Oh, Big Nick's gettin' old, hah? Maybe he'sa lose his grip. It ain't necessary tell Big Nick what'sa gots on any more."

"It's not that at all," Sophia Anastasis said.

"Who'sa this Ché Djilas, he'sa wanted so bad for somea rap down Earth-side Mr. Bader he'sa willing to trade a hun'd million for him?"

"Ché Diljas isn't one man, it's a whole operation. Sometimes we send one man, or even woman, to handle the situation, sometimes another." She looked at Rex Bader. "Shouldn't we send him out while we talk about this?"

"Mr. Bader he'sa stay. Evert'ing is on the up and up between Mr. Bader and Big Nick. What'sa operation is this?"

"Uncle Nick, you're doing fine up here in Satellite City, but we're running into difficulties, Earth-side. Every year that goes by new government restrictions just about everywhere in the world are giving us headaches. Last year, Common Europe nationalized the liquor industry, all except wine. Supposedly they compensated us but that won't take care of the yearly profits we used to make on our distilleries alone. This year the United States is threatening to double the capital gains in real estate investments. We've got a lot in real estate."

"What'sa this gotta do with this son va bitch communist, Ché Djilas?"

Al Rich put in hurriedly, "Nick, we do fine in the Bahama Islands. We own them, lock, stock and barrel. We own the government. But they're not big enough. We've got to get some new bases, some big bases . . ."

"Like Brazil," Rex Bader said mildly.

Al Rich glared hatred at him.

"Shud up, Al," Big Nick said. He looked back at Sophia Anastasis.

She said, "But Al's right. What with the United States, Common Europe and the Soviet Complex sewing up most of the world, we've got to find new fields in which to operate. Some of these countries, like Brazil, like India, are naturals. The people are frustrated. They aren't catching up with the advanced countries quickly enough. Just a push would topple their governments. You know how small a group Lenin and his Old Bolsheviks were? Possibly fifty. And there were a few thousand of the rank and file members of the party. But they pulled it off and assumed power. They weren't as organized, didn't have the resources, nor even the numbers we can throw in. But the country was ripe and they were able to sway the people into backing them."

Nick's large brown eyes had narrowed dangerously. "What'sa percent for us in bring a communist gang inta power in these'a countries?"

"Not really communist, Uncle Nick. That's just the excuse to get the people to follow, to help overthrow the current government. Then our people are in. It's not hard to put over. After a few riots and strikes and so forth, one of us, calling himself Ché Djilas, gets to the top men, or most of them. With the kind of money we can command, it's not hard to bribe even a Field Marshal or a President. They get on the air and surrender, saying that the revolution gives them no chance but to abdicate. Then they take off for Switzerland, or Satellite City, here, and retire. And we take over. At first we grant a few reforms, land to the peasants, a minimum wage, that sort of thing, until we're really entrenched with a good secret police and a good military machine. Then we start doing like Stalin and his clique did in Russia. We eliminate the elements that might stand in the way, those starry-eyed eggheads and idealists who supported us during the revolution. And then we really take over."

Sophia Anastasis leaned forward. "Don't you see, Uncle Nick? It would be the biggest operation we ever undertook. We'd no longer have to operate in countries like the United States and Common Europe with all their taxes and restrictions. We'd have our *own* country."

Rex Bader cleared his throat. "It'd be a big operation, all right. My government, that of Common Europe and the Soviet Complex as well, figure it'd wind up with World War Three."

Big Nick looked at him. "They do, hah? That'sa why you're here? They sen' you, hah?"

"Yes." •

The Syndicate head looked at Al Rich. "How come nobody he'sa told Big Nick about this'a big operation, hah?"

Sophia Anastasis took over again, smoothly. "Uncle Nick, that's one of the reasons I came up. To talk things over with you. Some of our associates down Earth-side think you ought to reconsider retiring. Some of them think perhaps you're out of touch, living up here. For instance, they don't think so much of turning the legal ownership of the Satellite City Authority over to one person . . . Cousin Gina."

Gina Angel, evidently amused, went over to the bar and mixed herself something.

Big Nick looked at Al Rich. "And you agree wit' these'a guys, hah, Al?"

Al Rich was flustered. He began to speak.

"Shud up, Al," Big Nick said to him. He breathed deeply. "You was one of these wise guys played this Ché Djilas, hah?"

"Well, yes, Nick. On several occasions. In Trans-Africa, for one place. It was easy Nick. A few riots in the streets and then we paid off the presidtnt and a few of the bigwigs and they all took off, abdicated like, and our group was in."

The old, old man's shrunken lips worked. For a moment, his sagging eyelids covered his eyes. Then they opened again. He looked at Sophia Anastasis.

"Al, he'sa crazy son va bitch, tryin' to pull off a operation right under Big Nick's nose. I don'ta know about you. Listen. I wan'a tell you why everything she'sa in Gina's name. Yoh don' know about the old days Sophia. Old Nick remembers these'a old days, hah? Big Nick he'sa ended them. In'a old days when some Don of a family, he'sa die, usual he gets hit, then all the soldiers in his family they'sa fight to become the new Don. Tommyguns, pineapples, all the rest, hah? When the Chief of the whole Cosa Nostra he'sa die, then there'sa really big blast, hah? Maybe hun'reds good family members they'sa get hit, hah? Big Nick ends all that. No more hittin' family members, hah? Since Big Nick is Chief there'sa no more war between the families."

So much talk had exhausted him. He took his time regaining his breath.

Finally, "Big Nick he'sa hang on for a long time, hah?" He glared at both Sophia and Al. "And all this'a time, he no goes'a soft in'a head. But what happens when Big Nick kicks off, hah? Who'sa takes over being Chief? I tell you who'sa takes over Big Nick'sa job. Nobody."

Sophia Anastasis and Al Rich startd at him.

"Everything she'sa in the name of Gina. Eva'body he'sa gotta cooperate with Gina, or he'sa out. Gina she'sa cooperate with ever'body cause she'sa can't handle it by herself. Everybody they'sa cooperate with Gina. No trouble."

Al Rich blurted, "Suppose something happens to Gina?"

Gina Angel said sweetly, "My will reads that in case of death other than natural, the Satellite City Authority, and all my holdings in International Divtrsified Industries, goes to charity. If I die a natural death, I have left it in the hands of the Reunited Nations what to do with my properties." She smiled and touched a finger to her lower lip. "However, it's unlikely that I'll be dying very soon, what with the health facilities up here. Perhaps in my older age, I'll change my will to fit the conditions that apply then."

Al Rich let air out of his lungs,

Big Nick said, "Now, this'a matter of Ché Djilas. That'sa out. You're'a crazy, both of you. You hear what Mr. Bader, he'sa said. The United States, all the rest'a the big countries, they'sa against these'a changes. These'a changes cause too much trouble. Okay, maybe Diversified Industries they'va got lots'a troubles these'a days, but we still got a good operation. And, like'a always, we'va been able to adopt. Thats'a good word,

231

we'va been able to adopt. This'a world, she'sa go on and what'a ever she'sa happen nexta'a year, we do our best, hah? We'sa smart. That'sa why we'rea still here. But none of this'a Ché Djilas crap. That'sa crazy. We bring ever'body down on us."

He snapped on the sole phone screen on his desk and said into it, "I wan' Mariano DeLuca, Cesare Agrusa, Pasquale Santino, down Earth-side. Scramble."

The three of them sat there and stared at him. For the time, he sank back into his chair and panted his breath. His heavy gray tongue came out and licked the shrunken lips. However, when the screen lit up he seemed to swell and his voice took on a firmness that thus far Rex Bader hadn't heard before.

Big Nick, his brown eyes flat, said, "Cesare, Pasquale, Mariano. This Ché Djilas t'ing. It'sa out, un'erstand? Anybody don't like it'sa out, hit 'em. Just'a like the ol' days. Hit 'em. It'sa ver' important." He flicked off the phone and turned back to Rex Bader.

"Okay, Mister Bader. It'sa all handled. You go back to your boss, hah? You tell 'em there'sa no more Ché Djilas. No more trouble. Satellite City, she'sa wan' no trouble with'a no Earth-side governmeit."

Rex hissed softly between his teeth and shook his head, as though with regret. "They wouldn't take it, Mr. Mangano. I need a fall guy."

The old man breathed deeply. He said, "What'sa matter with you, hah? You hear Sophia. There is'a no Ché Djilas. It's lotta guys."

Rex Bader looked at Al Rich and said, "They wouldn't believe that. They'll want somebody we can hang the label on. Al here, is one of the guys who played the part. We have some witnesses who evidently saw him when he was operating in Trans-Africa, some of the victims of the revolt."

"Why, you bastard," Al Rich rasped.

"Shud up, Al. Let me think, hah?" Mangano got out.

In a sudden rage, Al blurted, "Think! Why, you old has-been. You haven't been able to think for . . ." He brought himself to an abrupt halt and his eyes bugged. "I . . . I'm sorry, Nick."

"Don't call me Nick, you son va bitch." The old man must have touched a button with a foot.

Two men materialized. Rex Bader hadn't even seen through which door they had come. He recognized the type. So help him Hanna, they looked as though they had come directly from one of the historic gangster films of long decades ago. Their right hands were inside their jackets.

Big Nick said, "Salvatore, Tony, we'sa having a little trouble with'a Al. He'sa going down Earth-side with'a Mr. Bader, here. Mr. Bader, he'sa good frien' of Big Nick. You boys, you be sure you do everyt'ing Mr. Bader he'sa say, hah?"

Neither even bothered to answer. One made a motion of his head to Al Rich, who staggered from his chair, his face pale.

"Nick . . ." he pleaded.

"Shud up," Big Nick breathed. "I say just'a one last t'ing to you, Al. You remember the code of *Omerta*, the code of honor and silence, hah? You don' talk, Al. *Omerta*, the oath you take when you first become a man, hah?"

The three left the room.

Big Nick looked at Sophia Anastasis with his live brown eyes in their parchment face. She bit her lower lip and her cool had left her.

Nick Mangano flicked on his phone screen. He said, "Miss Anastasis, she'sa going to stay with us awhile. She'sa can go anywhere she'sa wan'. She'sa can do anyting' she'sa wan' to do, but she'sa not leave the hotel, hah?"

Sophia Anastasis came to her feet and said bitterly, "So, I'm sort of a hostage. There are a lot of our people that aren't going to like this, Uncle Nick."

He gave a weak snort of rejection to that. "Pretty soon, they'sa like it, or else, Sophia. Now, you shud up and get out."

She left, after taking time out to glower at Rex Bader, and then at Gina Angel, who took it with a smile, a cattish smile, but a smile.

As she left, Dominick, the guard at the door, entered, his ugly face in scowl.

He said, "Nick, I didn't want to bother you, but . . ." he held out his hand which contained Rex Bader's knife. "I took this off Bader." He jerked his head at Rex. "And he said it was a knife. But it ain't." He laid it on the desk before his chief and hesitated.

"Okay. That'sa all, Dominick."

When the bodyguard had left, Big Nick poked the supposed boy scout knife with a forefinger, then lookup up at Rex. "What'sa this, Mr. Bader?"

"A gadget to allow me to get through the locked door to the casino."

Gina Angel chuckled.

Big Nick nodded. He was obviously becoming desperately tired with all this. "What'sa really happen when you hit the casino for the big one?"

"I gimmicked the birdcage the night before."

"And whatsa happen to Rocky and that Russian guy, hah?"

"Rocky walked in on us. The Russian was my . . . partner."

"Ah ha, so he hadda die? How come?"

"To dispose of Rocky until I could finish my pitch with you. Rocky would have queered it. Evidently, Ilya blew the two of them out into space. He couldn't get rid of Rocky without going himself."

"He did it hisself, hah? He'sa willing to die?"

"As he said," Rex Bader said softly, "he was expendable. The world can't stand another arms race, winding up finally in another war."

The old man sank back into his chair, exhausted.

Rex said, "Do you mind if I use the phone screen?"

It was Gina who said, "Go right ahead."

He phoned, earth, Greater Washington, the Octagon and John Mickoff and when the other faded in, somewhat surprised, Rex said, "I've got Ché Djilas. Have some men meet us at the spaceport at Beni-Abbes," and flicked off the set before the astonished other could reply.

He said goodbye to Big Nick, who didn't answer, and Gina Angel led him to the door.

There, she touched a finger to her lower lip and said, as though grudgingly, "You're quite a man, Rex Bader, and with more of that integrity than I really thought."

He looked down at her and said, with his rueful grin, "Will you marry me?"

She flashed her white teeth at him, just as ruefully. "Thank you, kind sir, but we of the families only marry within the families. You should understand how complicated it might be otherwise, over a few generations. Besides, this particular girl is fated not to marry at all. All hell would break loose, considering that I hold the community property in my name, if I had a couple of children who legally were in a position to inherit. No, kind sir, I'm afraid you are looking at a life-long spinster."

"Then we'll never see each other again?"

"I didn't say that. You've still got a considerable amount of that twenty-five thousand pseudo-dollars in your account. You can always come up for a lost week-end. I never did teach you the *Noir* roulette system." She cocked her head up at him. "I just love lost weekends."

Aftermath

He was seated, in sheer pleasure, in his new apartment, a book in hand, a whiskey and soda on the table next to his comfort chair. On the walls were various prints and paintings and shelf upon shelf of volumes he had always wanted to own personally. The living room had a *spacious* feeling he loved.

He was living the life of which he had long dreamed.

The identity screen on the door hummed and he leisurely put the novel down and went over to open up. There were two strangers there. One of them brought forth his pocket phone and flashed the identity card set into the cover.

"Department of Internal Revenue," he said. "You're Mr. Bader?"

"That's right. Come in, gentlemen," he said hospitably.

When they were in the living room, Rex said, "Drink?"

"We're on duty."

"Okay. Great. Have a seat. What can I do for you?"

The one who had already spoken, said, "Mr. Bader, you haven't reported all of your income for this year."

"Yes, I have."

"Not according to our records, Mr. Bader."

Rex Bader said impatiently, "Look, I had precious little income beyond the almost quarter of a million mark-francs and pseudo-dollars I took in as a reward for capturing Ché Djilas, and that was tax free."

The thus far silent one nodded his head. "Did you hear the news. He hung himself in his cell this morning, before they could get him on truth serum. But it was Djilas, all right."

The first one said, "We realize that your reward money was tax free, Mr. Bader, but that's not what we're talking about. The news has gone around the world, a special story syndicated by a Mr. Ericsson, that you won one hundred million pseudo-dollars gambling in Satellite City. Ordinarily, we would have no record of such winnings. But on checking the story we have found several witnesses that saw you make your killing. You haven't declared the amount. Mr. Bader."

"Look," Bader said. "I never collected it. I supposedly won it, but gave it up. Among other things, I realized you Internal Revenue boys would simply strip me of practically all of it anyway."

The two of them stared at him in utter disbelief.

The second one said, "You mean you expect us to believe you won a hundred million pseudo-dollars and simply told them to keep it?"

Rex Bader cleared his throat unhappily and said, "Yes."

The two of them stood.

"I think you'd better come along with us, Mr. Bader, and explain to the chief about winning a hundred million pseudo-dollars and not bothering to pick it up."

Rex Bader blurted, "But I'm pledged to complete silence on the subject both to the Satellite City Authority and various governments. It's all very hush-hush."

"The first said smoothly, "I'm sure you are, Mr. Bader. I'm sure it is. Very hush-hush. Do you mind getting your hat?"

"Oh Lord, give me strength," Rex Bader muttered.